A DEED UNDONE

A DEED UNDONE

Robert Seymour

Courtley
procedures

First published 2017
Courtley Procedures
4 Waltham Way
Frinton on Sea
CO13 9JF

Phototypeset by Agnesi Text, Hadleigh, Suffolk
Printed and bound in Great Britain
by EAM Printers, Ipswich, Suffolk

A catalogue record for this book is available from the British Library.

ISBN 978-1-9998188-0-7

This book is dedicated, as always, to my wife Jane (who thought of the title); and to fellow Samaritan Jill, who gave me so much invaluable practical help in revising it, and to Carol, for her freely given encouragement and support.

This book is a novel; a work of fiction set against the background of a Samaritan Branch based in London that has never existed.

All the characters depicted in the story are also fictitious and any resemblance to real persons living or dead is entirely coincidental.

Although I am a Samaritan volunteer myself, the book does not seek to present the current aims, principles and practices of that organisation in any official sense. I hope, though, that it does reflect my pride in what all volunteers seek to do in helping callers and an appreciation of all their hard work.

ROBERT SEYMOUR

Author's Note

Why did I decide to write this book? To explain, I need to go into my personal history a little.

In mid-2016, I was diagnosed with pancreatic cancer and after a busy life following my retirement (particularly as a Samaritan volunteer) I now found I had much more time available to me.

Previously, as a Samaritan, apart from normal duties, I had become involved in other Branch activities. At one time, I had been a member of the Committee, served as a member of the Training Team, become a Leader, and was also involved with Data Protection issues.

Some of these activities, including normal duties, I was no longer able to undertake, so I thought: why not write a book about Samaritans? It is an organisation I had grown to cherish, particularly as represented by my own Branch at Colchester, which had brought me so much pleasure and fulfilment for six years since joining the Branch in 2011.

Better still – why not write a novel? This would give me much more scope in plotting the book and add drama to a work of fiction.

There was another reason too.

During my illness, I had become aware of what it must feel like to be on the other side of the fence.

One day, I was admitted to hospital for the night for urgent tests. I woke up very early the next morning and lay awake unable to go back to sleep. Fortunately for me, my loving wife was visiting later that day and was likely to be taking me home.

But what if I'd had no wife? Or partner? What if no one was going to come at all or, at best, a reluctant relative feeling under a family obligation to visit?

Then, I would undoubtedly have rung Samaritans, knowing that, even at four o'clock in the morning, somebody would listen to me and share my loneliness for however long it took.

So to sum up, this book is my tribute to the Samaritans who, in my view, provide a service that is not just unique but irreplaceable by any other charity.

That said, I also hope you enjoy the story for itself . . .

PROLOGUE

She stood up, swaying slightly as the soft breeze played on her face. A snatch of laughter reached her ears across the greensward – two adults were setting out a picnic while a boy and girl kicked a ball.

The time had come . . .

She walked across the grass towards the vastness of the sky, which beckoned her ever closer. She felt the tingle of the wind, suddenly harsher on her face. She inhaled the sweet smell of the grass, no longer smooth and even but growing in tufts at her feet as the earth began to fall away.

She reached the edge of the cliff, saw the emptiness below, and her arms began to flail . . .

GERALD

Gerald would never forget that day as long as he lived.

In the morning, there had been the monthly board meeting of his firm, Redland Capital Management, at Canary Wharf. It had gone well, reports revealing that the firm was in better shape than ever.

Gerald decided to indulge himself with a spot of shopping in one of his favourite places, Jermyn Street, a short distance away by taxi, thus avoiding the heavy business lunch with the other directors customary on these occasions, which he had given up in a desire to keep fit.

He loved buying treats for his family. For Mel, he bought perfume from Floris; for Scarlett, a jar of mixed sweets from Fortnum and Mason; and for himself a couple of new shirts from Hawes and Curtis.

Back in his office and well pleased with his purchases, Gerald was perusing the minutes of that morning's meeting when the phone rang.

Mel and Scarlett were dead.

The hum of the traffic outside stopped. The phone clattered on the desk. He stopped breathing for a few seconds, then blinked. His hand trembled as he picked up the phone again.

In Marblethorp, the sleepy Cotswold town where the Redland family lived, a young and inexperienced driver had lost control of his garbage truck, which had hurtled onto the crowded pavement, scattering pedestrians – save two, who were caught under the wheels of the truck.

Mel and her five-year-old daughter Scarlett had died instantly.

Gerald could not bear to remain in Marblethorp. He had moved, at least for the time being, into his London club, the Wanderers.

It had been bad enough having to stay in the house for the funeral and then the inquest, which had taken several weeks.

Gradually intense grief gave way to numbness. Gerald was existing in a kind of vacuum, unable to contemplate any real future.

With no family around him, he was completely alone in the world. From time to time thoughts of ending his life would pass through his mind.

Both his parents were dead. His mother had died when Gerald was a child. His father – the founder of Redland Capital Investment, based at Canary Wharf – had died some five years earlier of a heart attack. Mel's widowed mother was in a nursing home suffering from Alzheimer's, unaware of the death of her only daughter and grandchild.

For the moment at least, Gerald's business was running itself in his absence and his income was secure.

Club life suited Gerald. He could function within its routines and almost blot out everything else.

Tea was brought to his room at six thirty; he breakfasted between eight and nine and spent the morning reading the papers and periodicals in the Club Lounge. Then, promptly at eleven o'clock, he made his way to the Club Members' Bar. This was somewhere he could have his first legitimate drink – he had taken to sipping vodka from a hipflask in his room sometimes before then – and indulge in idle bar chat with other early customers if any were around. Eavesdropping on business talk that didn't concern him, accompanied by the gentle chink of glasses, soothed him.

And he could always talk to Harry, the barman.

There was something comforting about sitting on a stool in front of the bar, with its broad mirrors at the back making it look twice the size. The rich aroma rising from the deep leather chairs scattered about the room mingled satisfyingly with the faint hint of cigar smoke and alcohol that permeated the air, even when the bar was empty.

Harry was the perfect barman. He had a slight build and there was more than a hint of cockney in his soft voice. Good for tips on the dogs and horses, if that was your passion, or just general chat otherwise.

'Nice weather today, Harry.'

'Looks like the beginning of a warm spell. Usual, sir?'

Gerald nodded. Whatever you said to him, Harry could be relied on to talk exclusively in platitudes. There wasn't any need to make much mental effort. Gerald sipped his gin and tonic – the first of many – and mused.

Harry was right about the warm spell. Perhaps, before the alcohol really kicked in, it was time for Gerald to break out of the confines of the club and seek some fresh air, if such a thing existed in London.

Leaving the club, he walked down Pall Mall and Northumberland Avenue, before entering the Embankment Gardens next to the underground station.

He soon found an empty bench to sit on.

A few benches along, an elderly tramp delved into a rag bag of possessions and extracted a cluster of Special Brew cans. His odour wafted across on the breeze and Gerald wrinkled his nose in disgust.

Then he felt guilty. Was he so very different? Clearly he was much better off, but the slow descent into alcoholism would undoubtedly follow the same pattern.

As he watched the man slurping from a can, the deep visceral pain of bereavement once again struck like a sledgehammer. Away from the comfortable cocoon of his club, the raw reality of life overwhelmed him.

Once again thoughts of suicide entered his mind. But first, he needed to talk to *someone* about the tragedy, the pain – and it had to be *now*.

The he remembered a poster he'd often passed at Marblethorp railway station on his daily journey to work:

SAMARITANS

IF THERE'S SOMETHING TROUBLING YOU,
TALK TO US – WE'RE HERE 24 HOURS A DAY.

Gerald fumbled for his mobile phone, Googled the organisation and rang the number that came up on the screen.

'Samaritans – can I help you?'

The voice at the other end was soft, female.

Gerald dried up with embarrassment. Somehow, illogically, he'd assumed a man would answer the phone.

'Take your time and tell me, when you're ready, what's troubling you – there's no rush.'

The voice was soothing, gentle. Gerald gulped.

'I . . . I do need to talk to someone because – oh God, I've lost my wife and child . . .'

Gerald stood in front of his new house, such a contrast to the towering complexes of high-rise flats and office buildings all round it. The row of small terraced houses in Wapping had been preserved and attractively renovated, and looked out onto a pretty canal.

Gerald had bought 15 Cockpit Street, the end house, as an investment when the Docklands were being rejuvenated. Now it was ready for him to move in. It had all the basic furniture and amenities he required.

His new home also had the advantage of being conveniently near Canary Wharf, now that he had returned to work, at least part-time. Although he was still chairman, he had passed responsibility for the day-to-day running of his company to a managing director.

His plan for the next few months was to concentrate on his new home, to have further fixtures and fittings installed, and to shop around for more furniture, artwork and ornaments, visiting the antique markets in the area as the whim took him.

A pleasant breeze blew in from the nearby river as Gerald pocketed his house keys with a sigh of satisfaction. Having looked over the place, he now needed to explore the area for a local shop to buy daily essentials, although he intended to do the bulk of his shopping online.

But as it was nearing midday, it was time to find a pub and have some lunch first. He knew there were plenty on the riverside, including the Prospect of Whitby, so he began to make his way to that well-known hostelry.

For a while Gerald had rung Samaritans every day from the Embankment Gardens, where he knew he wouldn't be overheard. Different volunteers answered but that didn't matter, because just being able to talk of his grief on a daily basis to a stranger acted as a balm and had helped him to find a way to begin to come to terms with his tragedy.

Gradually, he'd begun to think about his future once again. He'd thrown away the hipflask, limited his consumption of alcohol to one gin and tonic at lunchtime and a half-bottle of Club Claret with his evening meal. He still visited the bar and chatted to Harry but now, as his mood continued to improve, he began to take more of a personal interest in the barman. He learned all about his mother's MS, the scrapes his wayward son was constantly having with the law and about Harry's real ambition, which was to save up enough money to leave the club and buy his own bar in Spain.

As Gerald strode through the streets on his way to the pub, he reflected on how his relationship with Harry had changed. He *listened* to him more now – something he supposed he must have picked up from the Samaritans, as they never spoke about themselves. Perhaps, as he was no longer needing to ring them for support, he should think about applying to train as a volunteer himself. Maybe that would be a way of repaying the debt he felt he owed them.

When he returned home after consuming a fine ploughman's lunch in congenial surroundings, he'd made up his mind.

On impulse, he tracked down the details of his local branch of the charity on the Internet. He found that Wapping Samaritans, at 48 Callabre Road, was situated not far from where he now lived. There was a phone number for prospective volunteers, and he promptly rang it.

A man answered, giving his name as Ambrose.

'All you need to do is attend one of our Information Evenings. No need to fill in any form at this stage. Just come in and we'll tell you what's involved. In actual fact, we're holding one tonight. Would you like to come?'

Gerald readily agreed. He wondered whether it would help if he did some preliminary research about the organisation before he went. Probably best to leave it, he concluded. He would learn much more about it at the meeting. However, on impulse, he did buy a short book about counselling at a local bookshop. It might come in useful later.

The Samaritans' premises were situated on the ground floor of a converted warehouse building. There was a lobby with comfortable chairs where Gerald sat with other people waiting for the meeting to start. He was impressed by how smart and modern the place seemed to be.

Samaritan posters adorned the walls. One in particular caught Gerald's eye. It showed a harassed young man who might well have been a student. Below the picture appeared the words written in bold, italic script:

You can talk to us about anything . . .

Gerald smiled to himself, remembering the poster at Marblethorp station.

Minutes after he arrived, a smiling, rosy-cheeked man emerged through a door controlled by a key pad and ushered them into a conference room. A projector sat on a large round table, ringed with chairs.

'Make yourselves comfortable,' the man said to the group, which was now about twenty-five strong. 'Hello, everybody – good to see you all here. Just to introduce myself – my name is Ambrose and I'm the Director of this Branch. Sounds very grand, that description of my role, but all it means really is that I'm responsible for managing the set-up here. The fact is that I'm a listening volunteer just like everyone else. We don't have grades of Samaritan or anything of that sort.

'Now, your coming here might be a first step in joining our organisation, but I suggest you put that out of your minds altogether for the moment. Just sit back and relax.

'I could talk about what we actually do for hours but then you'll only hear my side of things. Instead, I'm going to show you a film in which you'll not just see what we actually do but also hear from a variety of people who became Samaritans and, most importantly, *why* they decided to take it up.

'Help yourself to coffee or tea before we start' – he motioned to a table at the side of the room – 'then I'll play the film.'

Nobody in the group took up the offer, so he switched on the projector and pointed it towards a large screen on the wall.

Gerald had by now recognised Ambrose as the same man he'd spoken to earlier that day on the phone.

Among other things, the film made it clear that Samaritans was not just for people who were suicidal but for anybody who was going through a bad time and needed to talk.

As Ambrose had hinted, the volunteers who were interviewed on the film were all ages and from all sorts of backgrounds, but Gerald could see there was a common theme in what they were saying. Communicating over the phone as a Samaritan wasn't like normal conversation at all but was something much more specialised. It wasn't just talking; it incorporated an ability to really listen to someone and to share their space. Gerald realised that he would be required to learn a totally new skill from the outset. There were also pictures of the various types of premises the Samaritans used in carrying out their duties, which included receiving and responding to texts and emails, as well as answering the phone.

Ambrose switched the projector off.

'Thanks for listening and watching, everybody. Any questions?'

There were none and the group relaxed. A break was very welcome after having absorbed such a lot of information and coffee was suggested. Gerald felt rather embarrassed that he'd brought in his book about counselling, and slipped it onto a shelf beside where he was sitting, intending to take it with him when he left.

It was an opportunity to mix, and Gerald drank a cup of coffee with a couple of young men before the session resumed.

'Harrowing what we do in some ways, as you can see, but there's one very important thing. We all support each other – there has to be a second volunteer on duty with you always and you can share with them what you've heard if they're not on a call. On every shift, there's always a third volunteer on duty at home. At the end of a shift, you ring them to offload as well,' Ambrose continued.

'But don't worry about any of that for the time being. Think about what you've seen and heard, and whether doing this at all would suit you. It's not for everybody. Meanwhile, let me just tell you something about the application process. There is a form you'll need to fill in if you're interested, and we will obviously require all your details. We need to take up references too and do the usual police checks. If we take you on – and I must warn you there is an extensive training process to begin with – you'll be known only by your first name and assigned a number.'

Gerald shifted in his seat, stifling a sigh. *Bureaucracy!* Still, he supposed they had to be careful.

Ambrose then took them round the rest of the premises, but not including what he called the duty suite.

'That's where the phones are and our records. I can't take you into the suite because it's operational at present, and we have a strict confidentiality rule.'

Gerald also learned that, during certain parts of the day, the front entrance was left open and visitors could come into the lobby. To alert the volunteers on duty, they would have to press a bell, which rang in the duty suite. CCTV gave the volunteers a clear view of the visitor.

Leading off from the lobby was a visitors' room, where a volunteer and a visitor would be able to talk in private.

There were two sets of keypads. One for the door from the lobby to the conference room and duty suite, and another into the suite itself.

Having been handed a leaflet, Gerald sat down to read about the history of the organisation.

At the end of the Information Evening, the 'prospective volunteers', as they were called, were given the relevant forms to fill in, should they wish to apply. Basic disclosure checks would have to be made in the meantime. They were also told that the training would require them to attend eight sessions with two trainers on a succession of Sundays. Candidates were advised to think it over before they committed themselves, and interviews as to suitability would then take place.

Gerald didn't hesitate in completing the forms as soon as he got home. This was something he'd now decided he definitely wanted to do.

A few days later, a short interview took place at the centre with Ambrose.

After a fortnight, a letter eventually arrived. He'd been accepted for training!

Gerald wondered what he should wear for the training sessions. He'd noticed that most of the other prospective volunteers dressed casually, some in jeans and T-shirts, even in tracksuit bottoms. He didn't want to stick out but he was accustomed to wearing a suit and tie most days and he didn't want to look sloppy. After some thought, he decided to wear casual trousers, but to accessorise one of his Jermyn Street shirts with a plain blue cravat. They might be out of fashion but he still possessed a few and was conscious of an unsightly mole just below his neck line. He hated open-necked shirts anyway.

Training began almost immediately and took place on Sunday mornings. The number of people who had attended the Information Evening was now much reduced and the group that remained comprised only six people.

Gerald was glad about this because he felt that it would be easier to get on terms with each other in a small group. He was one of only two men in the group, the other being a student called Corin. The remainder were middle-aged women and a young girl named Lucy whose bright green trainers made her stand out.

He was to discover that she possessed a strength of character and resilience way beyond her years.

At the next session, the group was informed that two women had dropped out due to family commitments, which left just himself, Corin, Lucy and Daphne, a retired teacher.

The two trainers assigned to the group were called Lisa and Justin. Lisa was tall and graceful, with a manner that exuded calm. The bearlike Justin was physically her opposite, and he sported a luxuriant moustache. His voice, deep and gravelly, was the most attractive thing about him. Gerald later learned that he was an enthusiastic amateur actor.

One of the first lessons to be learned was about the Samaritan role, which had to be – to some extent – passive. In order to become a good listener, Gerald realised that he would need to set aside his personal thoughts and concerns.

He found it difficult at first. His own problems had a way of going round in his head, never really leaving him in peace, even when he was socialising. But, at Samaritans, concentrating on learning listening skills meant firmly trying to put such thoughts out of his mind. It also meant relating to his fellow volunteers in a new way. No longer should he think about other people – as he had always tended to do – in terms of wealth, background or age.

Gradually, Gerald began to learn more about his fellow trainees, particularly their attitude to some of the difficult questions that now faced them. The right to self-determination was to be a particularly troubling one.

It was Justin who broached this topic in the third session.

'It's a basic Samaritan principle that people must make up their own minds about deciding whether or not to end their lives. Of course, you encourage people to talk – but once it's clear that they *want* to die, never ever try to persuade them not to do it.'

Giving the group the chance to absorb this, he paused to sip a glass of water.

Gerald was taken aback by what had just been said, and reflected on his own situation. After he had lost Mel and Scarlett, the idea of ending his life had certainly gone through his mind at times, although it was no longer in the forefront when he'd rung Samaritans.

But suppose it had been?

Suppose he'd still felt desperate, on the very brink of doing something drastic?

'That leads me on to make a further point,' Lisa continued, 'one that sometimes can be difficult to come to terms with. Occasionally, a caller will want you to stay with them while they *actually* die.

To give the pills they've taken time to work, for instance.

'By this time, of course, you will have asked them many times to reconsider calling an ambulance, and it will be clear that they don't want any intervention from anyone at all. All they want is for you to stay with them on the phone. It's a natural human reaction – nobody wants to die alone . . .'

Gerald could see the sense of this last point but felt he *had* to query what had been said.

'Going back to what you said before, Justin, surely you should try and *stop* them? Doesn't everybody have a duty of care to prevent someone actually killing themselves?'

'No,' Justin said firmly. 'The decision to end their lives is always for them and you must abide by what they say.'

There was silence in the room while the group took this in. Lisa and Justin glanced at each other.

'Perhaps now is a good time to take lunch – we'll break for an hour. You all deserve a rest for a while anyway.' Lisa smiled at the group, reducing the tension in the air.

Three of them decided to visit a local café, leaving Daphne, who'd brought sandwiches, behind.

After purchasing some food, they sat quietly sipping their coffees. The café wasn't busy on a

Sunday afternoon, giving them the opportunity to talk freely.

While waiting to be served, they were distracted by a small child sitting at a nearby table with her mother. She was quietly mumbling nonsense into a feeding cup while being spoon-fed ice cream. All three smiled at the little girl's cuteness.

It was Corin, a rather intense, bespectacled young man, who spoke first.

'That little girl has all her life in front of her, and what she's got – what we've all got really – is so precious . . .'

His voice had turned into a whisper as he turned to face the others, tears in his eyes.

'I should know better than most. You see, my sister hanged herself in her bedroom. She was only fourteen. No note or anything, although later we found out she was being bullied at school. I actually cut her down and thought she might still be breathing. I tried mouth to mouth. I'd have done anything to save her. But I couldn't. That's why the idea of self-determination is really difficult for me . . .'

Lucy patted his hand.

'It's not surprising you feel that way, you know. Why not tell one of the trainers what you've told us and talk it through?'

Corin smiled gratefully, wiping his eyes.

'Thanks, Lucy – I might just do that when we get back.'

Gerald was staring at them both.

'Wait a minute, Corin. You did what any rational human being *would* have done, surely? Tried to save her – although it was too late by then. But say your sister had called you in first – the rope actually in her hand – and said, "I'm about to do it! Going to hang myself." If you apply the trainers' logic literally, it would mean you'd have to allow her just to do it – I suppose . . .'

He ended lamely, worried that Corin was looking distressed again.

'No – no, of course not. I'd run in to stop her . . .'

Gerald, feeling embarrassed, dropped his voice and said in an undertone, 'Of *course* you would. Anything else would be – well, inhuman frankly.'

It was Lucy who spoke up. Before joining Samaritans, she would have felt nervous about challenging someone like Gerald, a confident and articulate man of the world but things had changed.

'I don't think that's the issue though, Gerald. Of course, you would stop somebody *actually* attempting suicide in front of your very eyes! But that's not the situation the trainers are putting forward here, is it? Samaritans are there to *listen* to people – usually on the phone – not to advise or persuade them to do anything. That's the general principle they're on about.'

Gerald frowned. As a businessman and company executive, he was accustomed to assessing and evaluating things before making a final decision – so this went against the grain.

'I can't accept that – we must try surely and stop people from ending their lives – otherwise, why was the charity started in the first place?'

Back at the centre, Gerald waited while the trainers spoke to Corin first. Sensibly enough, prospective volunteers were encouraged to off-load their concerns in private when a particular aspect of training touched a raw nerve, as Lucy had predicted.

After a while, Corin returned, smiling tentatively, indicating that his anxieties had been allayed.

In the meantime, Gerald had re-examined his own thoughts, but concluded once again that the self-determination principle was, in essence, wrong. It was his duty to challenge it further, and he intended to argue the toss with the trainers.

So when they asked him whether he'd had time to reconsider his own position, he shook his head vehemently.

'I haven't – I *can't*, I'm afraid. To be honest, I'd have no compunction in talking someone out of suicide if I could! It *must* be the right thing to do – saving lives is our aim surely?'

Justin sighed. 'I thought it was already clear: as we can't advise people on how they should behave anyway, trying to get them to change their minds isn't an option. But, as your mind seems to be made up, there's a real stumbling block. Without accepting one of our core principles, you won't ever be able to qualify to join us as a volunteer, I'm afraid. Of course, there are other options – you might want to do a counselling course for example . . .'

Gerald felt a wave of irritation engulf him.

'I see – so no room for further argument about this then?'

Justin sighed again. 'Not in the circumstances, no.'

Lisa adopted a more emollient tone.

'Would you like to think about it, Gerald? We're about to end this session shortly anyway and you can always give one of us a ring before the next one.'

Gerald shook his head and rose to leave.

'No – I'm sorry, but I won't change my mind and I'd better go now. However, I do appreciate all the hard work you've put into the training, so thank you all the same.'

There was silence in the room after he left. Gerald's sudden departure had stunned them all, and it meant that their group was now smaller than ever.

Then Lisa said, 'That's it for today then, but we'll see each other again next Sunday. We may be down to three but that shouldn't matter as we'll be starting on role play in the next session.'

The trainers had explained earlier what this exercise involved. It meant that one of the trainees would act as a Samaritan, one of the trainers as a caller, and another trainee acting as an observer.

Lucy did wonder how Daphne, who appeared to be rather shy in company, would cope with this. The truth was that the latter hadn't contributed much to any of the discussions so far, nor made any contribution to the last part of the training.

LUCY

It came as no surprise to Lucy to be told the following week that Daphne had decided to drop out. After some thought, according to the trainers, she'd concluded that being a Samaritan was just too stressful, bearing in mind the responsibility that each volunteer had to bear. Lucy thought back to her own experience at college.

It had all begun when Lucy started feeling tired during lectures. Then she couldn't even get out of bed in the mornings or face the day. Eventually, a depressive disorder was diagnosed, forcing her to leave college altogether.

She lived with her mother in a spacious Barbican flat in the City of London, and soon found herself incapable of even going out.

At one point she'd felt so low that she'd contemplated ending her life by taking sleeping pills and anti-depressants, which had been prescribed by her doctor.

Her mother, Sue, was just too distracted by her work to be of much help.

In despair, Lucy contacted Samaritans after seeing a poster on a hoarding at a local train station.

SAMARITANS

THINKING OF ENDING YOUR LIFE?
NEED TO TALK TO SOMEONE? WE'RE HERE
FOR YOU, TWENTY-FOUR HOURS A DAY.
CALL SAMARITANS . . .

She'd picked up the phone, more nervous than she had ever been in her life.

A woman answered. 'Samaritans – can I help you?'

'I don't know. I . . . I . . . just feel so desperate. I need to talk to someone. There's really nobody for me . . .'

'You sound really upset, so just take your time. There's no rush at all. When you're ready to talk, I'll be here to listen to you. Remember that everything you tell us is confidential too.'

'Thank you. This is so difficult . . . talking about what has been happening to me.'

There was a pause. Lucy half expected the woman to chip in and ask more questions but instead she simply sounded reassuring.

'That's absolutely fine. Take as long as you need. I'm here when you're ready.'

It was a struggle, but at last Lucy began. She found that, after an hour, simply talking about her problems to a kind stranger calmed her down enough to realise that she should seek professional help.

Shortly afterwards, she contacted a doctor, and was referred to a skilled psychotherapist who specialised in Cognitive Behaviour Therapy and within weeks she was much less lethargic, and able, at least, to carry out daily tasks.

By now though, she'd missed most of the college year, although the authorities agreed that she could start afresh again the following September.

As a baby, she'd moved with her parents from Cardiff but still retained a slight Welsh lilt to her voice.

She was nineteen, blond with creamy skin but rather flat features that accentuated her large grey eyes. She was the only child of parents who had set up a small hotel chain in the outer London area.

She was four when her father died of cancer and her mother, Sue, had taken over the business, showing a determined and ruthless side of her nature that had never surfaced before.

Lucy was aware of the irony, because from an early age she suspected she might be a lesbian and if anybody was cut out to be a stereotypical example it ought to have been her mother, not Lucy herself.

Lesbians were strong domineering women, weren't they? Hell-bent on making their own way in the world; proto-feminists. At least that was the tabloid view.

But Lucy's mother, not averse to the odd casual relationship, only ever had affairs with men.

Lucy was the diametric opposite of her mother. She was dreamy, interested in the arts and fascinated by history; her ambition had always been to become an academic at college somewhere – or, failing that, a teacher.

When she experienced sexual feelings, sometimes last thing at night or first thing in the morning, the images that came to her mind and caused her to touch herself were those of women or girls. But she had not yet fully accepted what she thought must be her sexual orientation.

She had had the usual crushes on teachers at her secondary school – not that that was unusual, except that they had focused exclusively on women.

Then there had been Bella, the girl at university. Close friends – until Lucy had tried to kiss her after that party . . .

It was the end of term, and the whole class had gone on a pub crawl, ending up at Bella's flat having Irish-coffee nightcaps. Lucy had fallen asleep and had woken to find Bella draping her with a blanket and propping up her head with a pillow. They were now on their own.

Lucy had reached for her friend and hugged her. It had then seemed the most natural thing in the world to kiss . . .

Bella's disgust when she realised what was happening inevitably led to the end of their friendship.

All this had probably contributed to Lucy's eventual illness.

The fact was that she wasn't prepared to admit her sexual feelings to anyone, and certainly not to her mother.

Or even to herself really. She knew she was pretty, attractive enough to the many boys who asked her out.

As time went on, she might change, she told herself. 'Coming out' – a phrase that was constantly in the media – was something she would never have the courage to do.

Her mother wanted Lucy to follow her into the family business, which was why she had taken up a Business Management course at City University, London.

In order to fill in time before going back to college, Lucy had taken a job as a part-time assistant in a local sandwich bar catering for office workers.

Meanwhile, she tried to concentrate on catching up on her original course work, but soon began to fret again. Did she really want to continue with her present course? The truth was that she didn't really know what she wanted to do. A gap year might have helped but her mother was dead set against it.

Sue had shaken her head vigorously when asked. 'Lucy, you've got to get back to college as soon as you can and then come into the business. Vanser Hotels needs you, you know. Our prosperity depends on keeping the firm going.'

Lucy was alone much of the day as her mother was out at work. She missed having a father dreadfully, believing he might have been the kind of person to help her work through her problems.

Stuck at home, Lucy found herself spending too much time watching television or surfing the net. Some sort of voluntary work would suit her, but it needed to be more challenging than being a helper in a charity shop.

She cast her mind back to the kind lady who'd spoken to her when she had rung Samaritans.

How supportive she had been – just by listening. The fact that she was a complete stranger -- Lucy couldn't even remember her name – had itself helped enormously. Lucy had unburdened herself without embarrassment and thoughts of ending her life had been banished.

Perhaps volunteering for this charity might be just the thing for her?

Today Corin was absent as well, and that did take Lucy aback until Lisa explained why.

'Poor Corin developed acute appendicitis during the week, and was rushed to hospital. He'll be OK, but won't be able to resume with the group, although he fully intends to join the next training session. In the circumstances, we thought it would be a nice idea to send him a card – we've got it with us – would you like to sign it, Lucy?'

'Of course.' Lucy scribbled a message on the card, but then glanced up at the trainers anxiously.

'This means I'm the only person left in the group – is that a problem?'

Lisa patted her arm reassuringly.

'Justin and I have considered that, and had a word with Ambrose the Director too. There's no reason why we can't continue with just one person.

In some ways, it'll be better as you'll get one-to-one treatment from now on. But you must decide – we could stop the training altogether and ask you to come back in the future, but it would mean starting all over again, I'm afraid.'

'Oh no. I don't want to have to do that!'

Justin nodded.

'That's good. We'll start on the role-play part in a minute then. But first I need to reiterate something we've already touched on in training, and that's what we Samaritans mean by *active listening*. Really focusing on what the caller's saying and sometimes what they aren't saying. And remember to avoid giving advice, the absolute necessity of always being non-judgemental about other people's problems and, above all, remaining calm whatever the nature of the calls. That last bit could be particularly important when calls are abusive or sexually motivated. Does all this make sense, Lucy?'

'Yes, absolutely.'

'So, let's get stuck in with the first role-play session then.'

Both trainers used their acting skills to good effect. Lisa could pretend to be a distressed young housewife one minute or a lonely old woman the next.

It was now Justin's turn to act as the caller and Lucy as the Samaritan. In order to simulate a phone call, they took seats back to back.

'Samaritans – can I help you?'

'Ah, yeah. I need to talk to somebody. it's *really* difficult . . .'

Justin had disguised his voice convincingly to sound like a nervous teenager.

'Well, I'm so glad you've called us. Would you like to tell me what's troubling you?'

'It's just that . . . See, I'm sixteen and only just come out. I met this guy at a rave last week and he gave me an ecstasy tablet . . . Then . . . then we had sex. He was like one of the band's roadies, and didn't use a condom. I'm really worried that he might be HIV . . .'

Lucy thought for a moment. In a normal conversation, the temptation would be to chip in immediately and come up with advice. But that wasn't the Samaritan way.

'Could you tell me a bit more? Was there anything that he said that made you think he might be HIV positive?'

'No . . . but like we sort of talked when we met up. He's had lots of partners, he said and . . . and he really liked me . . . God, I'm so worried.'

He began to sob.

'Take your time. I can understand how distressing all this is for you. Have you thought of telling anyone? A friend, family perhaps? But I can understand that might be hard.'

'My parents don't know I'm gay, see, and me dad would kill me if he knew.'

'But you're only sixteen. Your parents will have to be told, won't they? Aren't you still at school?'

'Stop!' Justin was back to his normal voice. He turned around and gave Lucy a wry smile.

'Sorry, Lucy. You were doing so well up till then, but you started telling him what to do. And you sounded judgemental – it's so important not to. Remember, you're just there in the caller's corner, as it were. Listen and explore options sometimes – but beware your normal instincts. This is a different skill.'

Sometimes, Lucy found that their role-play sessions were really difficult. As the course continued, she speculated why she had embarked on this journey in the first place. Was she being altruistic for all the wrong reasons?

Generally, Lucy distrusted people who displayed overt altruistic tendencies – 'do-gooders', some of whom, she suspected, just did it to feel satisfied with themselves.

In the end Lucy concluded that she was doing something that fulfilled her, gave meaning to her life and, by its very essence – so many people needed just to talk to someone – was really important.

After basic training, when she began going into the duty suite with a mentor, she saw how the principles she'd been taught worked out in practice. The vital thing was never to be fazed. But because of the intensity of some of the calls, it was a struggle sometimes not to be.

In that respect though, the subtle tranquillity of the duty suite helped. It was such a welcome contrast to the hectic life taking place outside.

Her mentor was Ambrose. He explained some basic things about how the duty suite worked.

It had been adapted according to a design common to many Samaritan branches. There were three desks with phones for the Samaritans on duty, in booths, glass walled on three sides to minimise the sound. Only two were being used at present due to a shortage of volunteers. On the other side of the room, two more desks contained reference books that included lists of other branches.

When the centre was open and operational, another Samaritan, called the Leader, was also on duty at home. He or she was a more experienced volunteer there to keep an eye, or ear, on what was going on in the centre but also, and more importantly, to hear about the calls the volunteers had received during their duties. This offloading process between volunteers was considered vital in maintaining the emotional well-being of the branch.

Lucy was greatly relieved about the way this worked. Until then, she'd begun to think that the strain would be too much for any one person to bear alone.

During her first duty with Ambrose, Lucy listened to him as he took calls. When Ambrose wasn't occupied with a caller, Lucy also listened in to calls taken by Morag, Ambrose's duty partner.

Morag had dark red hair, done up in a bun, and a flushed complexion. She talked quickly in conversation, but her voice on the phone to callers was completely different. She sounded so calm and measured. Lucy envied her.

All the time Lucy was conscious of the fact that, at some point, she would be asked whether she was ready to take a call on her own . . .

The moment was to come sooner than she expected. She had assumed that Ambrose would want her just to listen in for another complete session, but towards the end of their first duty together he turned to her.

'Next time, after we've started and the phone rings, I'll ask if you want to take it. But only do it if you feel ready. Remember, just keep calm, you have all the time in the world to spend with the caller. What's so important is that you don't sound like somebody from a call centre. I'll be listening in, and may pass you the odd note for guidance.'

So, at the start of the new session, Lucy was ready. She took a deep breath, preparing herself for her first call.

But the session proved to be frustrating at first.

Although his phone rang constantly, all the calls turned out to be 'snaps'.

Ambrose explained. 'That's when the phone rings but the caller doesn't say anything. Men get more of those than you women, because the callers often want to speak to a female for sexual purposes. Nevertheless, it's always important to wait a while before putting the phone down. It could simply be someone summoning up the courage to speak and finding that very difficult.'

A few minutes later, Ambrose's duty partner that day, a young girl, motioned him over. There was a query about an entry made in the record book. Lucy had been taught that each call had to be logged and each entry in the book checked by another volunteer.

While Ambrose was dealing with this, his phone rang again.

Lucy's hand hovered over the receiver. She bit her lip. Now was the time.

'I'll take it, Ambrose.'

'Are you OK?' He mouthed.

She nodded and picked up the receiver, her hand shaking slightly.

'Samaritans – can I help you?'

'Oh, for God's sake, not a bloody bimbo,' said a drunken voice.

'I . . . You're through to Samaritans. We're here to offer you emotional support . . .'

'Yeah, yeah sure. I do need to speak to some-one, because, God, I'm depressed – but not to some bloody dolly bird.'

Tension was making Lucy's voice sound shriller than normal. She took a deep breath, determined to remain calm.

'I'm not a dolly bird,' she said defensively, and immediately realised it was the wrong thing to say.

There was a chuckle at the other end of the phone accompanied by a glug and a slurp.

'No need to deny it. Normally, I would love to

talk to you. In a bar, at a party, but this is different. I'm desperate. I want to end my life . . .'

'Would you like to tell me more about why . . . why you feel that way?' Lucy had steadied her voice and was beginning to feel more confident.

'Are you going to tell me not to do it?' The man's voice became harsh. 'What the fuck would you know about what I've been going through . . .'

Lucy didn't respond, ignoring the provocation, and thought back to one of the basic principles of training: self-determination.

'Samaritans never tell people what to do. We believe everyone should take responsibility for their own lives . . .'

'Responsibility! What? Are you some sort of specialist in that field? For God's sake, I thought I'd get through to somebody who might help me talk this through! You're useless!'

The phone slammed down at the other end. Lucy replaced the receiver. She was stunned. Ambrose was beside her, waiting for her reaction.

Where had she gone so wrong? She'd followed all the guidelines for handling this sort of call, hadn't she? Perhaps she might have over-reacted when he called her a dolly bird but that remark had really stung her. Maybe she just sounded too young over the phone.

Was she really up to doing this? She burst into tears.

Ambrose gently touched her arm. His face was creased with concern. He said, 'Take a break, Lucy. We'll come off the phones for a while and have a drink in the kitchen.'

After she'd taken the first sip of her drink – black coffee with plenty of sugar in it, the way she liked it – she talked through everything the caller had said and how he'd made her feel.

'That was a nasty one for a first call,' said Ambrose. 'You handled it as best you could. We're not machines, and sometimes what callers say gets under our skins, however long we've been here.'

Lucy dried her eyes.

'I'm ready to go back.'

'No. I think we should leave it there until the next session. No virtue in rushing things at this stage.'

Over the next few weeks, Lucy's confidence grew as she took more calls, soon without the need for Ambrose to mentor her.

Most of the calls weren't from people who were suicidal, but they might be facing trauma or crises of some sort in their lives, and needed to talk.

This really meant that Lucy had to develop the special Samaritan listening skill in its purest form. Often, that meant saying as little as possible, or even nothing at all, rather than something that might upset the caller or interrupt their thinking. Many of the callers were seeking reassurance and felt the only way of achieving it was to talk confidentially to a complete stranger. What they were actually doing was sorting out their own problems, finding different ways to look at themselves and their lives. In some ways the input of the listening volunteer was minimal, peripheral, yet somehow at the same time it was vital to the process.

There were many inappropriate calls too. Some were overtly sexual and Lucy had learned to bring those to an end as soon as possible.

Lucy vividly remembered her first.

'Samaritans – can I help you?'

'Oh, you got such a lovely voice, you have. What's your name?'

'Er . . . Lucy, how can I help?'

'Just by talking, Lucy. Just keep doing that. Guess what I'm holding in my hand?'

Lucy felt a wave of alarm.

'Please . . . I don't want to know. Samaritans are here to offer emotional support and give people the space to talk about their problems . . .'

'Yeah, you're doing that, love, and no mistake. Just keep talking. I'm about to come . . .'

'If you're masturbating, I'm going end this call.'

There was a sigh the other end. Lucy slammed the phone down.

Lisa, who'd been listening in on this occasion, smiled and patted her shoulder.

'Well done, Lucy. You couldn't allow that to go on and were right to end it when you did. Just one or two things – you sounded a bit shrill, and, if you can, it's best simply to tell him that you find the call inappropriate before you put the phone down. And never slam it! After all, we mustn't show anger towards our callers. That chap might ring again and be genuinely suicidal next time.'

Some calls of this nature were even more disturbing, Lucy found. They might involve fantasies with sexual overtones, with a clear manipulative feel about them. Lucy disliked these most at first, feeling alternately disgusted or upset by what was being said. She discussed this with Lisa, who reassured her that most volunteers found these calls difficult, but the best way was to talk about the calls to the Leaders.

'There's something else that's important too,' she added. 'Have a break and don't take any more calls until you've calmed down. It's always important to be at your best for the next caller, which could be someone in the act of taking their life.'

There were other kinds of abusive calls too, where people were rude and unpleasant just for the sake of it, or occasions when they needed to vent their frustration on someone – and a Samaritan volunteer who was trained never to answer back was ideal.

Lucy was pleased when she was told that Morag would be her duty partner on her first night duty.

'I'm quite satisfied that you're able to take calls on your own now. So I shan't be there when you do your first night duty, but Morag will keep an eye on things and make sure you're all right,' Ambrose had said. 'It's unlikely, but remember that we're all human and sometimes our own bad memories can surface because of what we're told by callers. Somehow, in the middle of the night, it can all seem so much worse. Morag will be there to support you, in case you need it.'

Lucy did feel nervous when she came on duty at eleven o'clock for her shift, which would last until six in the morning, but was reassured to see Morag already there, looking calm and relaxed, dressed in a pair of comfortable-looking slacks and a baggy jumper. The two volunteers still on duty before them were in the process of packing up, so Morag made Lucy a cup of cocoa as they sat in the kitchen.

'A great comfort drink at night. The sugar gives you energy,' Morag said, sipping from her cup.

Lucy laughed, her nerves making her giggly.

'That's really good, because I love sweet stuff, but can I munch chocolate instead?'

'Whatever you prefer. Do remember the most intense calls tend to come at night time. Mind you, you also get lots of calls from drunks, people looking for sexual gratification and sometimes people with mental-health issues as well. Those can be difficult as often the callers just don't make sense.'

She leaned over and patted Lucy's knee.

'This is your first night shift. I'll be there to help you. So, if you need me, but not immediately at that point, just give a slow wave through the glass partition. I'll come and listen in, as soon as I can. If it's really urgent – say someone's actually in the process of trying to kill themselves – then tap on the glass. I'll end my call as soon as I can, so that I can be there to support you.'

The other two volunteers, having finished their duties, came into the kitchen.

'Hope you have a good night,' one of them said.

Morag motioned towards the now empty booths.

'So off we go. By the way, have you been to the loo? That's very important because some calls can go on for an hour or longer.'

Lucy readily agreed with Morag's suggestion to turn the duty suite's main lights off, leaving only the reading lamps on in the booths. It gave the premises a more intimate feel, Lucy thought, and added to the calm atmosphere that she had found such an important element in being ready for calls.

At the start of the night, all the calls seemed to come from drunks, who either shouted abuse at her or make lewd suggestions. She was no longer fazed by this, just waiting as she'd been taught to end them as quietly and calmly as she could. This would never be immediate – all callers had to be given the benefit of the doubt – sometimes, drunks and sex callers could be suicidal too.

Then calls started coming in from people who couldn't sleep – kept awake by pain or worry.

Lucy knew that these were often from people ringing at perhaps the lowest time of all in the daily cycle of the human psyche: between two and four in the morning.

By four-thirty, Lucy was beginning to flag. There'd been a lull in calls, and she looked longingly at some armchairs at the side of the room.

So tempting to leave the phones and try and catch a nap in one of them. But she thought better of it. She knew she would be groggy and grumpy if she was disturbed.

Instead, she joined Morag in the kitchen and made a mug of strong black coffee. Morag was humming quietly to herself. She smiled at Lucy.

'You know, I had a really satisfying call just now. Just talking really helped the woman I spoke to. She wasn't suicidal, just feeling extremely low and finding it difficult to sleep. She had lost her husband a couple of years ago, still misses him desperately and this always hits her at night. She's quite well off, lives in a nice house and sees her grown-up children regularly too. So far they've been supportive, but now think that she should be over the worst. After all, he'd been sick for years so his death came as no surprise. Friends too feel that it's time for her to move on.'

'She's obviously still suffering a lot, but was she suicidal?' Lucy asked.

Morag shook her head.

'No, not at all. She would never contemplate doing something that would hurt her children or indeed grandchildren, she's so fond of them all. She just needed to offload and I hardly said anything. That's often the case – people don't really want us to chip in and, in those circumstances, the less we say the better.'

Back in the duty room, the two sipped their coffees. Lucy's tiredness had gone – instead, she felt a strange other-worldliness as she looked round the duty room. Cocooned from the world, it was almost as if they were on a spaceship hurtling through space . . .

Lucy's phone jangled, jolting her out of her reverie. She hurriedly put her mug down.

Morag put a hand on her arm.

'Keep calm, dear – make yourself relax. Remember: one of our greatest strengths as volunteers is the ability to radiate tranquillity, so that the callers feel they can say whatever they need to us.'

'Hello. What's your name then?' a man's voice barked.

Lucy remembered something she had been told in training. Someone asking for your name straight out might well be a sex caller hoping to establish a level of intimacy through an exchange of names.

She wasn't going to give him her real name. 'Lauren. What can I call you?'

'Hello, Lauren. My name's Joey.'

There was a rustling sound and the caller lowered the tone of his voice.

'I'm in prison, see. Fucking lonely stuck here in Seg and ready to do meself in.'

Lucy remembered what they'd been told about prison calls in training. Cooped up as they were for many hours of the day, prisoners often asked to speak to Samaritans just for a diversion. Mobile phones were illegal in prisons and generally prisoners were only able to use the public phones on the landings. However, some prisons did supply specially adapted phones just for Samaritan use.

Lucy also knew what 'Seg' meant. She'd heard this explained by Ambrose when he took a call from a prison. Prisoners could be placed on the Segregation Wing for an infraction of the prison rules.

Lucy had also been told that many such calls were to obtain sexual gratification. *Was this one such call?*

'How can I help . . .?' Lucy suddenly realised that this was the wrong thing to say. 'Er . . . what seems to be troubling you?'

There was gasping and more rustling sounds.

'Help, love . . . Yeah, yeah, you're doin' that an' all. Fucking voice is really turning me on. Go on, just keep talkin' while I come.'

Lucy pushed her feelings of disgust away. Her instinct had been right. The caller was using her for his own satisfaction. But now she knew exactly what to say.

'I'm not here to help you masturbate. What we offer is support, so this is an inappropriate call and I shall end it now.'

After putting the phone down she wondered whether she'd sounded too pompous, despite dealing with the call in a textbook way.

Time for a break and another coffee perhaps?

But, as it turned out, her next call drove all other concerns from her mind immediately.

Melanie's husband had died suddenly only six months before. She had a grown-up daughter who was as supportive as she could be, bearing in mind she was busy bringing up her own family, including twins.

After they exchanged first names, and a rapport was being built up between them, Melanie revealed her reason for ringing.

Melanie

It *might* be benign. That was the first thing that went through my mind.

Lumps in the breast weren't unknown in the family. Mum had had several over the years and in the end it wasn't breast cancer that killed her but advanced kidney disease.

Jody too had found a lump when she was in her first year at uni. She hadn't done anything about it either, until she'd come back that Christmas and told us. False alarm too, just a mass of fatty tissue that had been removed in a jiffy at the hospital, but Tom had been furious, telling her she should never leave these things for so long.

Surely I'd had my fair share of bad luck recently. Tom's sudden death of a stroke at sixty-two had come completely out of the blue – and he'd had a complete health check the week before.

Now the lump . . . it was situated to the side of my left armpit, quite low down, which was probably why I hadn't noticed it before. The doctor looked at it briefly and I saw the look of concern on his face, although he tried to hide it. He sent me off for a biopsy and arranged for our local hospital to do it as soon as possible.

I'd come home and poured myself a brandy but that hadn't really helped. I'd never been much of a drinker and the alcohol just made me feel morose.

I needed to talk to someone – but who?

Jody was too busy. The twins were teething now and keeping both her and her husband awake at nights. There was Alice, of course, but I'd phoned her so often just after Tom died that I felt I couldn't impose any more.

Then I remembered – something I'd read about Samaritans that had caught my eye in passing. Words set out in bold black type on their poster came back to me:

**TALK TO US AT ANY TIME YOU LIKE –
ABOUT WHATEVER'S GETTING TO YOU.**

I checked online for a contact number and rang the number given for the local branch.

My heart sank when a female voice answered the phone. The girl sounded much too young to understand the problems of a middle-aged woman like myself.

Samaritans – can I help you?

Overcome with embarrassment, I found it diffi-cult to speak.

'Take your time, and only when you're ready, tell me what's troubling you. There's no rush – we understand it can be difficult to start,' The girl said gently.

I felt so reassured by her tone that in no time all my worries and fears came tumbling out. It was such a relief to get everything off my chest. The girl introduced herself as Lucy and it wasn't long before I felt a warm connection build between us.

After a bit, I mentioned the biopsy and that I was waiting for the result with trepidation.

'How do you feel you'll be able to handle that?'

'I must *know*, mustn't I? The worry is whether I reported it to the doctor in time. Then I'll have to think about telling Jody and Alice if the lump turns out to be cancer . . .'

'You know, if you like, we can always arrange to ring you again. That would mean a volunteer from this branch ringing you on the actual day of the result – the evening perhaps, just to see how you are and the way things turned out. It wouldn't be me but it would be somebody who knows the background. I could leave a message for them.'

I turned this over in my mind for a moment.

'That's a very kind suggestion but I'd prefer to contact you myself if I need to talk to someone again. It's just so good to know that I can do that at any time, day or night, as you told me earlier. I'll leave you in peace now, Lucy. Thanks so much for listening and for your help tonight . . .'

Lucy

Lucy felt uplifted by Melanie's gratitude and how much more positive she sounded by the end of the call.

Exhausted, she made her way home by bus. The journey seemed so odd: most passengers had their day in front of them but she was going home to rest. As it was a Sunday morning, the café wasn't open, and she could stay in bed.

She soon fell into a troubled sleep, with worrying dreams coursing through her mind and which she couldn't remember when she woke up. It was a relief to get up at midday, and make herself something to eat, but it didn't prevent her feeling depressed and anxious again. Night duty was obviously a huge emotional strain and she wondered whether she could cope with it in the long term.

By the time another night duty came round, she was beginning to feel more confident. As other, more experienced, volunteers had told her, coping with duties did become easier as time went by.

Even so, a sense of apprehension tingled in her as she entered the building that evening and she greeted the volunteer she was relieving, a man called Ted. She asked about the previous calls. Had any of them been wildly different from the norm? By this time, at just before eleven, her night-duty partner, Anthea, was already on the phone.

Ted gave her a wry grin.

'Usual crop of people well under the influence of alcohol, but nothing of any real significance really. Well, I'm off. Have a good one!'

After he left, it was quiet for a while. Lucy had to stop herself yawning, despite having taken a nap earlier in the day.

A few calls began to come in but they weren't very satisfactory. One caller spoke so softly on a bad mobile connection that Lucy had to admit she couldn't hear her, at which the caller rang off abruptly. Another complained bitterly about a noisy neighbour playing loud music and demanded to know what Lucy intended to do about it. When she explained that Samaritans was a listening service not able to offer any practical advice, that caller rang off too, muttering abuse.

After a while, Lucy decided to make herself a coffee, strong and sweet as usual, to keep herself awake. Anthea came off the phone and joined her in the kitchen.

'Phew,' she said. 'I've just had Sarah on – you know, the lady who suffers crippling back pain, usually at night. Keeps her awake most of the time, she says. The trouble is she'll exhaust that topic, which is fair enough, but then switches to another, just as you think she's going to finish, and *then* begins to complain about the way her daughter treats her. As a result, the call can go on forever.'

'But you did manage to wind it up in the end, didn't you? It can be so difficult to do sometimes.'

Anthea sighed. 'You do have to be pretty firm eventually, and gently hint that you've been chatting for a very long time, and it might be time to bring the call to a close. Even that doesn't always work though.'

Before Lucy could reply, her phone rang.

'Samaritans – can I –'

'Please, please – just stay with me.'

It was a girl speaking fast, panic underpinning her words.

Relaxing her shoulders, Lucy took a deep breath and spoke calmly.

'Of *course* I will – just take your time . . .'

Silence.

'Would you like to tell me what's troubling you?'

'*Please,* just stay with me.'

'That's fine, I'm here as long as you need me . . .'

She tried a different tack.

'My name's Lucy by the way. What can I call you?'

'Willow.'

'Hello, Willow. Just to say you're through to Samaritans. How can I help you?'

'It's me dad . . . But it's really hard for me to start . . .'

'That's no problem. I'll wait until you're ready.'

'He sleeps with me and I hate it . . .'

'How – how long has this been going on, Willow?'

Silence.

WILLOW

Hot and sunny days are the worst. Why is every-body so happy when I'm not, and never can be?

Because they're from 'normal' families and good weather raises their spirits. Children play laughing in the park and mums and dads walk arm in arm, lapping up the sunshine.

But these things don't apply to us – that is, Dad and me.

There's only ever been the two of us since Mum died ten years ago when I was eight and I've been comforting Dad ever since. To begin with, we just cried together but when I reached thirteen, it became much more than that . . .

One night, he wanted more than a kiss and a cuddle and, even if it hurt at first, I let him do it – it gave him so much pleasure. He then swore me to secrecy. If anyone ever found out, he told me they would send him to prison and I'd never see him again.

That was only the start.

I know it's wrong but I can't stop it happening

any more. He thinks I never really minded and so I hate myself now and want it all to end . . .

Dad will be shattered but he'll find someone else soon. Nobody will ever know our secret.

Today is as good as any to do what I have to. Better really, because of the weather, which makes me feel so low anyway. Also, Dad's away in his lorry tonight doing a long-haul job.

I've got all the pills lined up. The sleeping tablets and the anti-depressants should do the trick. I've been hoarding them for weeks, fooling the doctor, and there should be more than enough now, when I take them with a half-bottle of vodka . . .

But I haven't got the guts to do it on my own. So I got the Samaritans number off my phone and rang. I just needed someone to talk to . . .

LUCY

'Willow,' Lucy continued softly, 'please – when you're ready, can you tell me when it all began?'

Silence. A lengthy pause.

'The pills are waiting for me.'

'What are you going to do with those pills, Willow?'

'Just stay with me, that's all.'

Then silence again. Lucy waited, but after another minute, decided to be more direct.

'Willow – are you thinking of ending your life?'

There was no answer.

'You don't have to take those pills, you know. I'll be here as long as you want.'

A gasp followed by a sigh and then the phone went dead.

WILLOW

After I ended the call, I lay on my bed, still in jeans and sweatshirt, thinking.

I'd hoped that this girl with the kind voice would just *stay* with me but instead she was trying to *stop* me.

I reached out for the pills . . .

Lucy

A few moments passed before Lucy put the phone down.

Had she done the right thing? Told Willow what to do? Might she have taken those pills and ended her life? Lucy would never know for sure.

She felt drained. It was time for her to have a break and call the Leader to offload.

'I think I said something I shouldn't have,' Lucy told Justin. 'She might have thought I was telling her not to take the pills.'

'You have to accept that we all make mistakes – if that's what it was. You gave her a piece of advice in the heat of the moment. That happens to all of us from time to time. The important thing was you explored the question of suicide with her, didn't you? Just try and put it out of your mind, if you can. Let's talk about it again in a few days' time when you've had a chance to think it through.'

'But I'll never know *what* Willow actually did. Did she end her life? Or take an overdose that didn't actually kill her, but that might have left her really ill, only for her to die later? Or, might she have changed her mind?'

'Speculation is pointless, Lucy, because as listeners we hardly ever know the outcome of calls. I don't want to sound flippant but you'll just have to learn to live with it. If it keeps preying on your mind, don't hesitate to give me a ring later. I'll be home all day.'

ALISON

Alison Hock had never felt so nervous as she did that day. She'd been told to be at the Old Bailey well before ten o'clock, although there was no indication as to when her case would actually begin.

Just sitting outside Court Number Two where the trial was listed was terrifying enough in itself. God knows how she would feel when she actually had to enter the court and give evidence.

The grandeur of the great hall of the building. with its biblical scenes painted high up inside the cupola, pressed down on her. In particular, she noticed one of the axioms written in bold black ink which lay underneath.

Right lives by law and law subsists by power . . .

She shivered.

Perched on a hard bench just outside the court, she fiddled with a handkerchief and pulled her long chiffon scarf tighter around her neck. She loved scarves, drawing comfort from their gentle, reassuring pressure on her skin.

Her mother had a large collection of silk scarves, her choice each day matching not only her outfit but her mood.

Alison had played with them as a little girl while her mother dressed, loving their sensuous smoothness as she rubbed the material against her cheek.

Just entering the building had been an ordeal in itself. She had to go through security, which consisted of having her body patted down by a female official, who hurried people to move forward before searching their handbags. But at least the physical contact wasn't from a man.

'Can you tell me how to get to Court Two?' she had enquired of this woman after the search.

'Up those stairs in front of you, past the lifts on the right-hand side, straight through into the old part and it's in front of you,' the woman rattled off.

Alison couldn't be sure she had taken it in, but didn't have the chance to check. The bossy female was already patting down someone else. So it was hardly surprising she got lost and found herself outside Court Five, before eventually being directed to Court Two.

Alison noticed that Courts One to Four were rather different from the others in the rest of the building. She suspected that these old courts had been designed to strike fear into the wrong-doer and impress the majesty of justice on the observer, whereas the newer ones, like Court Five, were far more functional. She shivered and couldn't help feeling that she'd been transported back a hundred years to the days of hard labour and the death penalty. Although she was a witness, just sitting there felt like being on trial herself.

The hall had been virtually empty when she'd arrived, but as time went on more people strode past her, going either into the offices opposite the courts or into the courts themselves. She noticed that the ushers, dressed in black gowns, stood outside, speaking to individuals as they went in. Some robed people wore wigs too so she surmised they were barristers, their headgear making them appear rather intimidating. She rolled her handkerchief into a ball, anticipating being questioned by one of them. They all seemed to strut with a measure of arrogance, even the women – their wigs often perched on top of elaborate hairdos – and Alison wondered whether this was a deliberately acquired attitude, to emphasise the majesty of the law. The doors to Court Two, however, remained resolutely shut until a flustered usher arrived, holding a bunch of keys.

Alison felt that she should tell him who she was, wondering whether there was a room somewhere reserved for witnesses. As he was about to go into the court, she approached him.

'Excuse me. I . . . I'm a witness in one of the cases listed today. Do I . . .?'

The man turned and glanced at her irritably.

'Oh, for goodness' sake, they should have told you where to go when you arrived.'

'I just asked about where the case was listed.'

'No matter. You're early anyway, but all witnesses should report first to the Witness Waiting Area on the fourth floor. So I suggest you get up there as soon as you can.'

Minutes later, Alison had found the right place and was told by an official to wait until she was approached. In the meantime, she could purchase a drink from a machine if she wanted one and a lady from Victim Support would come to see her in due course.

The room resembled an airport lounge. From time to time, ushers came in, shouting names and escorting individuals out. A while later, a young woman, looking harassed, came in and spoke to the official who pointed to Alison. Alison noted that the woman was hugging a sheaf of papers to her and kept glancing at them as she came over.

'Are you Miss Hock?'

Alison nodded.

'Ah, good. I'm from Victim Support, here to support you. I have to tell you that we're terribly busy today – so many serious cases at the Old Bailey, you see and . . . and . . . I'm new too. Only taken on last week. So you're my first case as it happens.' Flapping her hands, she dropped her papers on the floor.

'What is it you actually do?' Alison wondered whether this nervous lady's presence would only make her feel worse when she came to give her evidence.

'Oh, sit with you now, if you want. Later, I can be in court too sitting behind the witness box. Of course, I can't speak to you during your evidence. That wouldn't be right.'

'But can't I talk about it with you afterwards?'

'Oh, no. You'll be warned that you mustn't discuss the case with anyone after giving evidence – not until the case is well and truly concluded.'

They both looked up at the official at the desk who was waving in their direction. The woman retrieved her papers from the floor and stood up.

'Oh, do excuse me –that chap on duty said there are several other people for me to see this morning. I'm not quite sure when you're due to give evidence, but I could come back later.'

Alison had made up her mind that she'd be better off coping on her own.

'No – that's fine. I'm quite capable of managing, thank you. I'm sure there are other cases where you'll be needed more . . .'

'Very well,' the woman moved away swiftly and Alison decided to buy a drink. She chose tea as the best option, although the tepid liquid served in a plastic cup tasted of little more than flavoured water.

As time rolled by and no one came to fetch her, Alison wondered what was going on. She'd been warned to attend the Central Criminal Court at 9.45 sharp so assumed her case would be listed that morning. Eventually, she approached the desk.

The official showed her the court list. 'I'm sorry, love. Your case isn't due to start until two. Change in the listing at the last minute – happens all the time. You can go off if you like, but be back here by half-past one at the latest.'

Alison contemplated leaving the building but decided to read her book instead. She'd abandoned the crime thriller she'd been halfway through, and turned to a light romantic novel bought earlier at the tube station. She couldn't face food before giving her evidence. As she'd slept so badly, eventually she did nod off but woke with a start to find the same usher from Court Two standing over her.

'Miss Hock, you're due on in five minutes. Just follow me please.'

Jolted out of her sleep, Alison felt a wave of panic. Any minute now, she would be confronted by *That Man*. She began to shake.

'Take several deep breaths first', the usher said, more kindly now, 'and "give yourself a moment". When you feel ready just follow me.'

They set off, eventually reaching Court Two, and Alison was bustled through the door and into the court. She could see the witness box in front of her, and the vast interior of the room. The walls were covered in oak panelling and it contained benches covered in dark green leather. An imposing figure dressed in scarlet sat on the bench. Alison caught her breath – she'd read somewhere that some English judges wore red, but assumed that most of them wore black as they did in the American crime dramas she liked to watch. He also had a bristling ginger moustache – just like her father's. She shuddered.

Standing at the back of the witness box, she became aware of voices in court. Nobody seemed interested in her at that particular moment, so the usher took the opportunity to whisper to her.

'You're in front of Mr Justice Midgeon. He's a High Court Judge, so senior to everyone in the building, save for the Recorder of London. Not known for his patience or charm frankly, so keep your voice up as much as you can.'

Alison counted to ten, forcing herself to calm down. One blessing was that at that point she couldn't see her attacker as the dock was on her right, obscured from her sight. Gradually, her breathing became more even. She drew the scarf ever tighter round her neck, feeling that, in some way, it might help to protect her from what was to come.

After a minute, the judge stopped talking and rattled off an instruction to the bewigged clerk who was sitting below the bench. After standing up, the latter said in a stentorian voice, 'Call Alison Hock!'

Alison approached the front of the witness box, looking round apprehensively as the whole court came into her field of vision.

At last, she saw him: Edward Trooper, the man who had raped her.

Thankfully, he seemed far away, half hidden by the large dock around him. Apart from the judge, she now saw several counsel on their benches, all robed in wigs and gowns, as well as other official-looking figures, some of whom were seated at a table in the well of the court. The public gallery was also crowded.

Another usher now stepped forward and thrust a Bible and card at Alison.

'Madam, please take the Bible in your right hand, and read the words of the card after me . . .'

Alison duly took the oath and felt herself swaying a little. She'd noticed a chair behind her, but nobody invited her to sit down. Moments later, she became aware of a barrister asking her a question. He seemed a long way away.

'Miss Hock – would you give the court your full name and address?'

Alison duly gave it, not daring to look at the questioner but staring straight in front of her.

Mr Justice Midgeon sighed as he turned in her direction.

'Really, Miss Hock, you must speak up! We shall need to hear your evidence, you know, so do speak as loudly as you can, although not too fast either, as I'm required to make a note. It might help if you pulled that scarf away from your face as it seems to be covering part of your mouth.'

She'd never felt as tense as she did now.

She'd fallen in love with Dr Ahmed Kalpa when he took up the position of junior registrar at St Raphael's where she worked as a nurse.

Ahmed was different from most men she'd come across. He was calm and gentle and seemed to enjoy just talking to her, when they saw each other during coffee breaks. Alison rather liked that he was different from the other doctors, more formal and quietly spoken. Being with her, though, seemed to bring him out of his shell, and it wasn't long before he asked her out, and their affair began. But there was never any future in their relationship. Ahmed wouldn't have left his wife and children even if he hadn't returned to Pakistan.

By this time, she was working as Mr Edward Trooper's theatre nurse and made the mistake of confiding in him after the affair had ended.

Edward was a much more flamboyant character altogether. His fair hair curled fashionably over his collar, matching his droopy moustache. He tended to wear flared trousers and generally sported a brightly coloured tie.

She and Edward were never really anything more than colleagues, but working so closely together, they did to an extent become friends. She'd never fancied him and indeed thought, as he was unmarried, that he might be gay.

All she'd done was to simply let her hair down that one night . . .

Edward was a heart surgeon. That day he had carried out a triple by-pass operation lasting several hours. Afterwards, to unwind, he and Alison had visited several bars in Soho and, daringly, she'd tried a variety of exotic cocktails. As Edward lived in Wimbledon, Alison had offered him a bed for the night at her flat.

It was true that the stress of the operation and the unaccustomed amount of alcohol had loosened Alison up a bit, made her giggly, playful even . . .

So she hadn't minded him taking her arm when they got out of the taxi back at her flat. True, she'd become more aware of his masculinity – heightened by the slight smell of perspiration mixed with the tang of his aftershave – and, true, she'd kissed him goodnight before leaving him to sleep on the sofa bed in her sitting room.

She'd been in a deep sleep, lying on her back, before being jolted awake to find him on top of her, just entering her body.

Horrified and screaming with shock, she squirmed away and kicked him out of her bed.

He bundled up his clothes and fled.

Now, she was being asked questions by the prosecuting counsel, who was taking her through her evidence swiftly and efficiently. She continued to be nervous and was repeatedly told by the judge to keep her voice up.

Later, the defence barrister, a middle-aged man called Trent, cross-examined her courteously enough but was relentless in his questions. When she hesitated, he always gave her enough time and space to compose herself, which lulled her into a false sense of security. He had a habit of never looking directly at her but always addressed the court as a whole, which also added to her sense of intimidation.

'Miss Hock, recently at the hospital, you'd been having an affair with one of the registrars, a Dr Kalpa, I believe.'

'Yes, but –'

'Is this relevant?' growled the judge.

'Indeed it is, My Lord. Goes to my client's state of mind.'

'In what sense?'

'Well, he had knowledge of it, as everyone did, I suggest. In fact, wasn't it common gossip amongst the medical staff, Miss Hock?'

'I don't know . . . but you couldn't keep anything secret in that place.'

'Quite. But that night in particular, you actually talked about the affair with my client, didn't you? Told him it was over?'

'Possibly . . . I did look on Edward as a friend.'

'Didn't you tell him that you missed the sex?'

'No! I would never have said that . . . I couldn't . . .'

'Can you be sure? Look at your witness statement.'

There was a pause as it was handed up to her.

Trent read a passage from it slowly.

'"I did have a great deal to drink that night. My recollection of what happened earlier that evening was blurred, and I'm not sure how we said goodnight. It's possible, I might actually have kissed him . . ."'

'Yes – but . . . a goodnight kiss, that's all. Then I woke up to find him on top of me. He was . . . he'd penetrated me. I never agreed to that!'

'Come on, Miss Hock. That was what you *really* wanted, though, wasn't it? This was entirely consensual intercourse. Isn't that the truth?'

'No!'

'Drink' – Trent adopted a wheedling tone – 'changed you that night, Miss Hock. You lost your inhibitions. Dr Kalpa had gone. You missed the sex and Mr Trooper was on hand. You led him on. He believed you wanted sex. You wanted it, too. Indeed, you actually invited him into your bed!'

Alison began to sob.

'It wasn't like that at all. It's true we'd had far too much to drink. It had been such a long and difficult operation, which is why we went out just for the one at first, but then – well, we were just letting our hair down. But I never asked him to sleep with me. Look what he did afterwards. He ran out of the flat . . .'

'Another lie, Miss Hock. He stayed until early morning and then left in the normal way to catch a tube home.'

'No . . .'

Trent consulted his notes.

'Well, let's turn to your conduct *subsequently* then. You were never medically examined, were you?'

Alison was baffled for a moment.

'No – but why should I have been? I had a shower immediately after he left – I felt so dirty – and . . . and . . . he hadn't actually hurt me physically.'

'What, even though, according to you, he had penetrated your body without your permission!'

Blushing furiously, Alison clawed at her scarf on the shelf in front of her that the judge eventually had made her remove.

'Only a *very* little way before I woke up and realised what was happening . . .'

'Is it necessary to pursue this any further, Mr
Trent? Haven't you made your point?' The judge
interrupted.

Trent nodded. 'So be it, My Lord. There's just
one other matter before I sit down. Miss Hock, why
wait three days before going to the police?'

'I was embarrassed. He was a colleague. I felt
ashamed. I shouldn't have got drunk in the first
place frankly and I should never have invited him
to stay the night. I suppose I dithered – but when
it struck me that, come what may, I would have to
confront him, I went to the police.'

'Or,' Trent hissed, 'having had second thoughts,
you regretted agreeing to sleep with him in the first
place and decided to *punish* him instead.'

'No. No! None of what you're suggesting is true.'

Later, Trooper himself went into the witness box.

Alison noticed that he'd put on a plain blue tie
for the occasion.

'I would never have contemplated sex with
Alison at all in normal circumstances,' he said, 'but
things were different that night. We'd both had a
considerable amount to drink and, at the end of

the evening, she invited me into her bed. Then we had sex.'

Alison couldn't believe what she'd just heard.

'He's lying. Surely they can see that!' she muttered to herself, as she sat at the back of the court.

The jury consisted of eleven men and one woman. They kept casting sympathetic looks towards the witness box – except for the woman, who glanced in Alison's direction from time to time, shaking her head. Alison felt a surge of hope – *somebody* appeared to believe her.

But in the end it made no difference. After receiving the majority direction – namely, that they could convict or acquit on the basis of a verdict upon which at least ten of them were agreed – the jury still acquitted.

Mr Trooper left the court a free man.

Still only twenty-five, Alison left her job in London and went to live with her widowed mother in Nottingham. An only child, she'd left home at seventeen and rarely returned, but then her father's death changed everything . . .

Her father had served in the Royal Air Force and had accepted a redundancy package. He'd been granted a reasonable pension and, with her mother's salary as a vet's receptionist, the family wasn't badly off. Alison's father hadn't really needed to find another job – not that he ever really looked.

Instead, he began to drink – at first in the local pub, then at home in the evenings too. Often, he would sit sozzled in his chair mindlessly gawping at the TV all evening, before staggering off to bed. Her mother, a keen bridge player out most nights, simply shut her eyes to there being any problem.

By the time she was sixteen, Alison had developed from a thin leggy child into a curvaceous teenager. That was when the problems had begun.

He father started touching her up, always when her mother wasn't home and never too directly; occasionally brushing against her bust or allowing his hand to stray up her thigh.

Then, when she grew older and started going out with her friends regularly, it got worse. Her father would greet her effusively, pushing his body against her and trying to kiss her on the lips. Alison decided to ignore it, putting it down to the fact that he was drinking too much, and not wanting to embarrass her mother. Besides, in all other respects, he was an indulgent parent, always giving her money when she asked for it.

That last night, after a party, she arrived home just after one o'clock in the morning, to find her father still up and sitting in the lounge, a half-empty glass of whisky clutched in his hand.

He leered at her, taking a swig from the glass.

'My little daughter, dressed up to the nines! Come in then, give your old dad a cuddle. I could do with a bit of affection.'

He grabbed her arm, pulling her towards him and giving her a slobbering kiss that narrowly missed her mouth. Despite being drunk, he was surprisingly strong as he pushed his body against hers.

'Come on, my lovely, give your old dad a bit of a feel.'

Horrified, Alison watched as he fumbled with his flies, pushing him away from her as forcibly as she could. He lurched backwards and as he fell he banged his head on a coffee table.

The shock seemed to bring him to his senses. Clutching his head, he staggered to his feet.

'Christ, Alison, I'm sorry. It's the booze and, well, the way you look now . . . Please, *please* forgive me and don't say anything to your mother . . .'

The very next day, Alison heard that she'd been accepted as a trainee nurse at St Raphael's teaching hospital in London, which meant that she was required to leave home immediately. She never did tell her mother what had happened but, after that, she returned home as little as possible and avoided being alone with her father at any time.

A few days after the rape case had concluded, her mother rang.

'Darling, it's Dad. He had a massive heart attack and he's dead! I . . . I can't believe it! He was only sixty-two. It's my fault – I knew he was drinking a lot and I neglected him – ignored him! He also used to complain he never saw his daughter any more and that you hardly ever visited, but I knew you were busy and just brushed it aside! Oh God, I feel so guilty. Can you come home?'

The arrangement was meant to be temporary, but after her mother fell ill with a progressive form of dementia, Alison nursed her until her death.

It seemed inevitable somehow, as she was a qualified nurse and could never quite banish her own feelings of guilt about what had happened.

She should have come home more often, to confront her father perhaps and persuade him to seek help or, at least, explain her attitude to her mother.

The end result though was that, by remaining at home all those years, she'd sacrificed a good portion of her life. Yet, by so doing, she'd also managed to blot out the terrible things that had happened to her in London.

As their only child, she inherited her parents' savings and with the sale of their detached house, which had greatly increased in value over the years, she found herself quite well off.

Free at last, she decided to move back to London. She felt she could never return to nursing but was determined, still fit and well and only in her fifties, to take up a new career.

She travelled to the capital, and chose the Docklands area to live in. It suited her mood as she attempted to make a fresh start, as it was a brand new development. Eventually, she bought a flat with stunning views of the Thames in a building that had formerly been a warehouse.

Once installed there, she would be back in the centre of things and able to indulge in all the cultural delights of the city: art galleries, museums and, her particular favourite, the theatre.

Over the years, her situation had forced her to shut herself off from the world. However, she'd granted herself an occasional treat and visited the Nottingham Theatre, at times when she could arrange for someone to sit with her mother. Now, she would be free to go up to the West End at any time and see any play or show she wanted.

But that wasn't enough. She was determined to find a job in London too.

Soon, the time came for her to move out of the Nottingham house.

A few days before the arrival of the removal men, she'd spent some time packing up all personal and family possessions, deciding what she wanted to retain, give to charity or discard altogether. She was determined to start in London afresh with as little clutter as possible.

She decided to keep a couple of paintings – not valuable in themselves but for sentimental reasons – before turning to the family photographs, contained in a number of albums as well as loose in a box.

She decided to keep an album of early pictures, mainly of herself as a child, but resolved to get rid of the rest, including all the loose photographs, except one of her mother as a young woman, and another of herself in her first evening dress.

Alison had looked so glamorous then, with her dark-brown hair back-combed and pinned in the chignon style fashionable at the time. Even taking into account the passage of time, her appearance was so different now. Her greying hair was much thinner and cut in a short bob.

As she shoved the box into a plastic binbag, another photograph fell to the floor. It was of her father, in his uniform as a Royal Air Force officer, taken shortly before he retired.

She tore this up quickly – his drunken conduct towards her, coupled with the rape and humiliating trial, had made sex anathema to her and stifled any desire on her part ever to seek another relationship with a man.

Once in London, she took up a secretarial/PA course in Holborn and swiftly found herself an ideal job working for the female executive director of a cosmetics company based in the City.

For a few years, she seemed to have put her past firmly behind her and was able to enjoy her new life.

But then Trooper's story hit the headlines.

Which was when she started to ring Samaritans.

LUCY

It had been a quiet morning duty when Lucy received her first call from Alison.

'Samaritans – can I help you?'

'Yes . . . I . . . well, you might . . . it's difficult to start,' the caller had replied.

'Take your time – we do understand that it can be difficult. There's no rush. When you're ready, perhaps you can tell me what's troubling you? What's on your mind?'

'I was raped . . .'

There was a long pause, which Lucy didn't try to fill. It was important for a volunteer not to chip in too soon, if at all. A pause gave the caller a chance to think about what they wanted to say next. Eventually though, Lucy had felt a bit of gentle probing was appropriate.

'I understand that this must be a very difficult time for you. Would you like to tell me a bit more?'

Lucy felt that what she'd just said sounded so inadequate. 'In your own time, of course. Take as long as you need,' she added hastily.

'It's so difficult. I tried to come to terms with it but . . .'

Lucy waited.

'It's that doctor – the one in all the papers – about what he did for that pop star. Saved her life apparently. Well, he's the man that raped me years ago!'

The story about Giona, the world-famous singer, had been splashed all over the tabloids. She'd been performing at an open-air concert in Hyde Park, attended by her thousands of fans, when she suffered a massive heart attack, just after performing her latest hit. Rushed to hospital, she'd been operated on at St Raphael's.

Mr Trooper, the heart surgeon on duty, saved Giona's life by carrying out an emergency bypass operation. It had been touch and go, as the singer's heart was discovered to be greatly enlarged, but ultimately, after many hours in theatre, it was completely successful.

Overnight, Mr Trooper became a celebrity and there was even a petition to try to get him a knighthood in the next honours list.

The singer's multiple fans had breathed a collective sigh of relief and the popular press had made the most of the story for a while.

'How do *you* feel about all the praise he's received for what he did?' Lucy asked.

'Oh God, it's so unfair! He may be a good doctor – I knew that anyway. But he ruined my life! He raped me – but nobody knows anything about that!'

Lucy recalled an interview with the doctor on a television news programme shortly after the operation. He'd been asked about his career, but nothing was said about him ever standing trial.

Surely, if he'd been convicted, that would have featured? Lucy thought.

She then asked what she immediately realised was an insensitive question.

'Did you report what happened to the police at the time?'

'Of course I did! But, by twisting the truth and telling lies, he got away with it – with the help of his clever lawyers! So I'm the one who takes the punishment! The rest of my life almost ruined – all because of him! It took years to get over it then, to put it behind me – but now this!'

'It must be really difficult to handle your feelings but, at least with us, you can talk about it. Everything you tell us is completely confidential, and you're in a safe and secure place to be able to do that, as long as you need to. By the way, my name's Lucy. What can I call you?'

'Alison . . . Thank you. Do you know it's so good to hear you say that. I can't talk about this to anybody else really. It's so embarrassing! I suppose people always wonder in rape cases, don't they? Was the victim really a victim? Or did she ask for it? Sounds crude, I know, but that's what people often think, don't they?'

There was some truth in that, thought Lucy, thinking about some of the lurid stories she'd read in the newspapers. Yet her first reaction was outrage on the caller's behalf and she couldn't help blurting out, 'God, that must be awful! Would people actually suggest that?'

Blushing, she stopped herself, remembering what she'd been told during training. Her personal view was irrelevant. She needed to concentrate on the caller's feelings, not on her own.

Instead, she reflected back on something Alison had said.

'I think you told me that before all the publicity, you had come to terms with what happened. Is that right?'

'Yes – yes. It did work for a long time, specially when I gave up nursing and moved away from London to look after my mother, which I did until she died . . .'

Lucy felt now she could ask a direct question: 'How did you get to know the doctor?'

'I was his theatre nurse. We worked closely together at St Raphael's. Friends too, I thought – but then he took advantage of me, didn't he? His story sounded so plausible at the trial.'

After she recounted all the details, Lucy asked, 'Can you think of any reason *why* you weren't believed? The judge, the jury . . .'

'Why? Well, the whole thing was weighted against me from the start, wasn't it! Even though I was a witness, I was marched into that courtroom and made to feel it was me on trial, not the defendant. Then there was that pompous judge – he intimidated me from the start! Even told me to stop fiddling with my scarf, which is something I've always done.' She began to sob. 'It was only a habit of mine, after all. Then the defence barrister – male, too, of course – began to ask questions. He twisted everything I said, and made it sound so false, as if I'd made it up.'

'Surely *someone* spoke up for you?'

'There *was* the prosecutor – but he didn't seem to care. He asked me what happened to begin with, it's true, but in a bored, indifferent sort of voice. I felt alone having to prove I was telling the truth . . .' She broke down again.

'You've been through a really bad time, Alison . . .'

'Thank you – yes. Oh God, I've got to go or I'll be late for work. Hope I can ring again and speak to you, Lucy. When are you next on duty?'

It was then that Lucy made another fundamental error, contrary to all her training. She knew that she should always deflect such a request. Samaritan policy was clear: never allow a personal relationship to develop between caller and volunteer, and avoid arranging future contact in this way.

But she couldn't help herself.

'Thursday morning, between eight and ten thirty.'

There was a pause.

'I'll ring you then at eight thirty on the dot. Can you be sure it'll be you?'

'I'll do my best.' Then she added recklessly, 'If it's not, just put the phone down and ring again. You'll get me eventually.'

She flushed red, knowing that what she'd suggested was absolutely wrong.

She also began to worry about another aspect of Samaritan policy. There was a general instruction that if a caller seemed be becoming too dependent on the service, then this should be reported to the Director, Ambrose.

There was a real risk that Alison might now be falling into that category. But Lucy couldn't help feeling flattered by the fact that the woman wanted to speak to her again, so she decided to do nothing.

ALISON

I felt a huge surge of relief. I'd made absolutely the right decision to speak to somebody about the feelings that had threatened to overwhelm me when I'd read about Trooper.

I thought I'd managed to banish his very existence for ever, but now the whole, horrible experience had been revived once more by seeing his name in print.

For so many years, just suppressing my feelings had worked but then I realised that I had to speak to someone about it for the very first time. But who should it be? I didn't need counselling or therapy, just a friendly ear – a total stranger whom I could trust to keep whatever I said confidential.

It was at this point that I remembered the Samaritan poster I'd seen on my way down to London.

And now, I had somebody I could talk to. Lucy might sound young, but her voice was soothing and gentle. I'd found a haven of comfort when I really needed it.

LUCY

Alison was ringing every week now, and almost always spoke to Lucy. Sometimes, it didn't quite work out – Lucy might be engaged with other callers throughout her duty slot – but mostly the arrangement seemed to work. Lucy now booked the same duty well in advance, and as her fellow volunteers tended to vary, suspicions were never aroused.

Gradually, Lucy felt that her relationship with Alison was changing in a subtle way. Alison might be the caller but her maturity and experience of life generally made Lucy want to confide in her. *Why couldn't they become friends*, Lucy thought, *even if it broke all the rules?*

But she tried to hold back, knowing that to self-disclose, and allow herself to talk about her own problems, would be taking an irrevocable step.

ALISON

One morning, I noticed that, despite her trying to hide it, Lucy sounded very depressed. I was determined to find out why. After all, she'd been such a help to me over the last few weeks.

'Lucy, talking over my problems with you has been such a help, and although I know it's not the done thing, I feel I should get to know you a bit better. You sound really down today. Why don't you tell me what's troubling *you* for a change?'

And so it all poured out – the pressure from her mother, her unhappy life at college – but I suspected there was something even more fundamental actually worrying her.

So I suggested we meet up somewhere, and do the kind of things Londoners never usually get round to. The tourist things that our capital city offers. What could be the harm in that? Even though I suspected that would be even more against the rules.

We made a plan to visit the National Portrait Gallery, somewhere neither of us had ever been, and that interested us both. It would be an appropriately neutral venue in which to meet before settling down to chat.

LUCY

Lucy and Alison spent the morning at the gallery, starting early, before the place filled with tourists. Visiting each room in sequence was a journey into history in itself. Lucy was particularly fascinated by the Civil War period: the bright silk clothing and exquisitely intricate lace collars of Charles I, contrasting with the craggy-faced Oliver Cromwell, clad in sombre armour.

They lunched in the crypt of St Martin in the Fields, shut up and forgotten for many years but now converted into a self-service eatery.

Once distinguished citizens had been buried there, and the floor was studded with gravestones dating back to the seventeenth and eighteenth centuries. Alison frowned as she tramped over them to reach a vacant table near the service area.

'Stepping over the dead seems somehow disrespectful, don't you think?' she said.

Lucy laughed. 'Not at all. Think of the people buried here. Wouldn't they be delighted to play an active part in life again? Even if it's only to provide a floor for this café. Have you noticed people actually look down and read their names? Better than being forgotten in darkness for evermore.'

Having found a table, they both chose chilli con carne – the dish of the day – and after drinking copious glasses of water to combat the strength of the food, they began to talk.

'Tell me more about your college life, Lucy. It doesn't sound as if you're enjoying it much.'

'No. But Mum said it was so important that I prepare the ground before going into the family business. Vanser Hotels: "small but significant home-from-home hotels for the discerning" – that's what it says in the brochure.'

Alison poured them both more water from a carafe.

'It doesn't sound as if you really want to go into it. Have you thought about what you'd really like to do?'

'Something involving history, which I've always loved. It probably comes from my dad. He'd been a teacher before he inherited Grandma's boarding house down in Cardiff. Mum was determined to do that place up, turn it into a proper hotel and then expand. Dad had to go along with it. She was the driving force in the marriage, always. I've often wondered whether it was the stress of running the business that contributed to his death. I'll never know, of course.'

'If you'd had the chance, what do you think he might have said about you going into the business?'

'Oh, well, Mum says he'd have wanted me to carry on the family tradition – but what tradition? Vanser Hotels, as a group, only really took off after Dad died. His life insurance helped. I . . . I think he would have wanted me to do something that I really cared about.'

Her voice trembled a little and she paused, taking a deep breath. Had she said too much?

'Go on,' Alison said gently.

'I only took the Business Management course at college because of Mum, but I knew it wasn't for me right from the start.'

Alison patted her hand.

'It's what *you* want, Lucy, that matters. Not what your mother thinks – although I'm sure she has your welfare uppermost in her mind. Don't you think you're being unfair to yourself too? Especially as you became ill recently. You need more time.'

Lucy sniffed. 'I did tell my mum that, but she insists that I go back to college and continue the course when it starts again. I was quite good at maths at school, which was why Mum said I should go for it in the first place. So I'll just have to lump it. I'm so used to Mum being in charge of everything – she had to be strong, I know, bringing me up on her own – so I just go along with it. Sounds pretty weak, doesn't it?'

'No.' Alison patted her hand again. 'Not for a moment. Look what you're doing for Samaritans. That shows you have real strength, you know – helping people emotionally. Now, I'm going to get the bill. This'll be *my* treat today.'

They arranged to meet again, and visits to the Tower of London, the Tate and Tate Modern soon followed.

Then, one warm, sunny day, they decided to venture outdoors and go for a walk on Hampstead Heath.

Afterwards, having stopped off at a café to buy some sandwiches and a couple of coffees, they rested on a park bench with a panoramic view of London, the tall buildings glittering in the sunlight.

The pond lay not far from them and the sound of the ducks quacking and the warm sun made them both feel drowsy and relaxed. For a moment, Lucy appeared to be falling asleep as she turned her face up towards the sun. But then she sighed and turned to face her companion.

'Alison, there's something I need tell you . . .'

Alison waited.

Lucy rubbed her mouth with her hand as if she was finding it difficult to come out with the words.

ALISON

I wasn't going to press Lucy any further. She'd tell me more in due course. But casting my mind back to the gallery, I wondered whether it might be something to do with her sexuality.

While we were there, a group of young students was behind us, accompanied by their tutor, who was giving a running commentary on the paintings. One female student stood out. She was lovely, with long black hair cascading down her back, and I couldn't help noticing Lucy giving her covert glances as the group followed behind.

Later, we visited the gift shop. While I was looking at the postcards, I turned round to see that Lucy had drifted away and once again was staring at the same girl, who was sifting through T-shirts in another section. The girl was giggling with a friend, tossing her glossy hair away from her face. I was curious.

'Do you think you know her, Lucy?'

She blushed. 'Oh no – it's just that – she's so pretty . . .'

It crossed my mind then that Lucy might be a lesbian. But no doubt she would tell me in her own good time.

Now back on the Heath, Lucy's voice trembled a little.

LUCY

———

'There is something else. Oh God, I'm the one who's supposed to be the Samaritan but I do need to get this off my chest. I've never been able to talk about this to anyone before, least of all my mother . . .'

She paused, turning her face up to the sun.

Alison waited. A mild breeze wafted over them, carrying the smell of newly mown grass. *Don't push her*, she thought. She'd learned that from Lucy, who had already told her that it was part of Samaritan training to allow callers time to unburden themselves.

'You can tell me,' Alison murmured. 'I've been around longer and, as you know, been through a lot myself, and, well, we're now friends, aren't we? So please do confide in me.'

'I really want to but . . .'

Two boys, chasing a ball, ran in front of them. The ball bounced up on the seat beside them. Lucy threw it back before continuing.

'*If* I do, I don't think I can go on treating you like a caller any more.'

Alison smiled. 'We've passed that stage now, Lucy. Anyway, you helped me so much over Trooper that I can cope with my feelings now. At least, the press have stopped praising him up to the skies. I suppose there's new sensational stuff to report. What do they always say about newspapers? "Tomorrow's fish and chips"? I don't suppose that, even with the Internet, things have changed that much.'

The sun disappeared behind a cloud, causing a chill in the air. Lucy shivered before replying, wishing she'd brought a jumper to wear as well as her fleece. The time had come to be completely frank.

'You see, Alison . . . it's . . . well . . . I like girls. I know that's no big deal these days and I'd come out if I could, but it's Mum. She'd never come to terms with it. Since Dad died, she's had several boyfriends – never anyone permanent, mind you, but she tells me about them all the time – even how they perform in bed. It's embarrassing really.'

'Does she ever ask about *you*, Lucy? Your feelings? Relationships, for instance? Have you had any?'

'Oh, I've pretended to have had the odd boy-friend, gone out with them a few times, but Mum's not really interested in me. Too wrapped up in herself.'

The sun came out again.

'Surely though, if you told her how you feel – that you're different from her – even be frank, and tell her you're gay, she might at least try and see things from your point of view. After all, you are her daughter.'

'That's the real problem. She thinks I resemble her in every way, because I've never stood up to her or even argued with her! But then, how could I? She was the only parent I had, you see.'

Her voice became bitter.

'It's really ironic when you compare our personalities. Mum – the thrusting, independent business woman – surely, she ought to be the lesbian? Not me – her placid daughter who just wants a quiet life.'

'It never works that way, Lucy. You are what you are. And nowadays, you can be completely open about your sexuality. It's your absolute right as a gay woman to strive for happiness and contentment, just like anyone else. You'll probably be much happier actually than someone like me. I don't hate men and I've never been attracted to a woman but I can't see myself ever wanting to be involved in any sort of sexual relationship again.'

'Oh, Alison, I didn't mean to bring it all back.'

'No, no. Don't get upset, Lucy. Each to his own. We all have different needs and problems. I do understand how difficult it must be for you over your mum, but surely you have to tell her, don't you? It's your future that counts, what you really want to do with your life and how you intend to live it. I did notice how interested you were in the artwork we saw in the gallery – the historical paintings and all that. Think about the things that really matter to you.'

She put her arm round Lucy.

A black cloud was beginning to hover over the Heath.

'It's getting cold. Let's call it a day now and meet up again soon. We've become friends now, surely? Meanwhile, I'll give you my phone number so you can put it in your mobile.'

Lucy searched the pockets of her jeans. *Damn* – she'd left her mobile on the kitchen table at home. 'Sorry, I haven't got it with me.'

'Never mind. I'll scribble it down on one of my firm's business cards.' Alison took one out of her purse and wrote on it.

'Meanwhile, while we're at it, give me yours too,' she continued. 'I'm off to a conference next week with my boss, but we'll meet again soon, I hope. Going out together like this is good for us both, I'm sure.'

It was the cover of the colour magazine that caught Lucy's eye that Sunday morning.

She'd walked to the newsagent's to collect the papers as she usually did when she saw it, although it wasn't part of the paper she normally bought for her mother and herself.

The magazine carried a full-page picture of a middle-aged, rather fleshy man in an open-necked shirt, grinning unctuously at the camera.

A caption read: *Celebrity surgeon tells all . . .*

Underneath in smaller type appeared the words: *For the full story of how the doctor saved the life of pop idol Giona – see inside and only in this paper. Read the first extract of his autobiography* Have a Heart!

Lucy wondered whether Alison had seen it and knew of the contents by now, as she settled down to read the inside of the magazine for herself.

ALISON

I was devastated when I first saw that article about Trooper. His face mocked me from the moment the paper, together with the magazine, plopped through my letterbox. I shouldn't have read it, of course, but I couldn't help myself, and that included the extract about his time as a doctor at St Raphael's. How much he'd enjoyed those early, challenging years as a heart surgeon and progressed from there to become a consultant.

And no mention of his loyal theatre nurse or, of course, any reference to the trial.

I had to get over it, and, now, there was someone I could confide in. Lucy. I would see her soon enough.

The next day, I went to work, feeling better. Work would sort me out and help me forget the whole thing – at least during office hours. Anyway, the trip to New York would be an ideal diversion.

Then Maura, my boss, came into the office.

'Thought you might like to see this.' She tossed a magazine down on my desk.

'I remembered you said once you'd worked at St Raphael's as a nurse. Did you ever come across this chap?'

'Vaguely,' I mumbled. 'Can't really recall . . . it's been some years now . . .'

Maura seated herself next to my desk.

'Funnily enough, I've come across this chap myself. He was at a charity dinner some months ago – one of those functions organised by the City Corporation for hospital fundraising. We were sitting at the same table. He was a good talker – passionate about his work as a heart surgeon, so I bet his book will be a good read. Then he goes and saves that singer's life too – the mag reckons he'll be awarded a knighthood soon. What's the matter, Alison? You've gone quite pale.'

My heart had begun to race and I could feel myself beginning to panic.

'Oh, I'm fine – just a slight headache . . .'

Maura was concerned.

'Touch of the flu perhaps? It's going round like wildfire at the moment, so Alison – don't hesitate, please – take the rest of the day off. We're off to New York the day after tomorrow, and we need you fit for that.'

But I knew that my sudden indisposition had nothing to do with the flu.

A few moments after Maura had left, the phone rang.

I lifted it, my hand shaking uncontrollably. Jamming it against my ear, I took a deep breath and tried to stop my voice from breaking.

'Hi, Alison? John here – John Chesser. Just to ask what time the board meeting is today. It's in my diary, but not the time.'

John Chesser was a non-executive director of the firm. I remembered him as a genial old buffer who attended meetings only twice a year.

'It's . . . I . . .' I couldn't get the words out, my hands now shaking so much that I dropped the phone, which clattered down the side of the desk.

My head began to shake as well as my hands, arms and legs. Feeling sick, I rushed out of the room, making it to the loo just in time before vomiting.

Would this happen again? Every time the phone rang, would I suffer a panic attack?

What if these sensations occurred when I was answering calls at home?

Maura was waiting for me back in her office. She must have heard me being sick.

'Alison, are you all right?'

I nodded. I'd already decided that my only course was to go home immediately. I'd try and see a doctor later to seek help with my nerves.

'You're right about the flu. I'll just go home. I think I'll get a cab. Can't face the tube, frankly. Oh, do you mind, Maura, ringing John Chesser back to tell him the time of the board meeting this afternoon? I . . . we were cut off when he rang before to ask.'

'I'll sort it out, Alison. You've gone as white as a sheet! Just sit down now and I'll fetch a glass of water. Also, I'll order a cab from here – no need to wait in the street.'

I sank down on a chair and sipped gratefully from the glass of water she had brought me, holding it firmly against my mouth to stop my hand from shaking.

After I arrived back home, I felt exhausted and went to bed, waking up after an hour feeling very much better. Perhaps there was no need to visit the doctor after all.

But then the phone rang, and once again I was seized with panic. I couldn't allow this to go on. I had to fight these feelings, so I forced myself to pick up the receiver.

It was Maura.

'Alison, how are you? Much better, I hope. Just confirming our arrangements. I'll pick you up at yours on the way to Heathrow. Say about nine. Flight's not leaving till two, but we can chill out in the Club Lounge.'

Panic seized me again. The traffic, crowds at the airport – it would be too much. But I forced my feelings down.

'Fine. Thanks, Maura.'

I made an appointment with the doctor straight away and went down to the surgery that afternoon.

I didn't really want to go into any history so simply asked for something to help me tolerate the nine-hour flight to New York, making out that I had a phobia about flying.

The doctor prescribed Diazepam, which I knew was a drug not recommended for long-term use any more, but that could be beneficial in the short term.

Knowing that the first challenge would be at the airport, I took a double dose before leaving home.

Maura had organised a chauffeur-driven car to take us to the airport. The journey and the security checks at the airport went remarkably swiftly and I began to relax. The Diazepam helped, and I made sure to put the remainder of the pills in my handbag.

We took our seats in the Club Lounge. It was still quite early, but Maura suggested that there would be no harm in us having a drink.

'A bloody Mary will perk us both up, Alison, and help you get rid of that flu bug too. I must say, you are looking better today.'

I nodded, smiling, and sat back to watch the mixture of humanity coming through the doors. There were businessmen clutching briefcases while talking into their mobile phones, prosperous-looking older people embarking perhaps on holidays of a lifetime, single people of all nationalities . . .

I froze. I couldn't believe it but an all-too-familiar figure was coming into the lounge.

Gone was the hair – he was virtually bald now but he was much older, of course, after all these years – and less substantial in the flesh than he had appeared in the photograph in the magazine. There was no doubt, however.

It was Trooper.

Worse still, Maura had spotted him too.

'Well, well – if it's not Mr Trooper, the famous surgeon himself.'

She watched him as he made his way towards some vacant seats. He was obviously on his own.

'I'll go over and ask him to join us. We got on so well at that dinner and I'd love to talk to him about his book. I'm sure he won't mind as he is trying to publicise it. You don't object, do you, Alison?'

How could I refuse?

'No. Sorry, must rush, caught short!' I babbled and rushed in the opposite direction to Trooper, where the cloakrooms were situated.

Inside a cubicle, I began to shake violently and scrabbled frantically inside my bag for the Diazepam. I had to calm down. There was plenty of time before our flight was due to be called. By that time, Trooper might have gone.

But what if he was flying to New York as well? I had to do something, talk to someone!

Lucy . . .

LUCY

Lucy was having a good day.

She'd bitten the bullet and taken Alison's advice and told her mum about her sexuality. Amazingly, her mother hadn't turned a hair.

'I suspected as much, Lucy. You never seemed that interested in boys. But I was waiting for you to tell me in your own good time. I had a crush on an older girl at school once but that passed and –'

'Mum, I've grown up now.'

'I know. What I meant to say was if you'd been younger, it could just be a passing phase, but as long as you're sure in yourself, that's what's important.'

Afterwards, Lucy sighed with relief. *That's one thing out of the way, thank God.* But she'd wait a bit longer before going on to talk of her career.

Later in the day, she'd gone to the centre to do an additional duty, as somebody had dropped out unexpectedly. For the very first time, she did a 'Face to Face', seeing someone in person who'd come in needing to talk.

It turned out to be a really rewarding experience.

A boy had come into the centre and asked if he could speak to someone. His name was Ben and he was aged nineteen, although a thin beard and pinched expression made him look older. He wore the dirtiest trainers Lucy had ever seen – originally blue but now almost black with dirt.

He'd been living on the streets for weeks since running away from his stepfather, who had been regularly beating him for years.

Trying to survive by begging, he'd begun to dabble in drugs and was worried that his habit might soon lead to crime and prostitution. He also missed his mum dreadfully and had begun to think that suicide might be the only way of escape.

As one hand kneaded the other, his voice broke.

Lucy plucked a tissue from a box and gave it to him.

'Well, the main thing is that you've come in here, after *such* a difficult time and talked to me. You're welcome to do that any time you like, by visiting us again when the centre is open or just ringing us. I'll give you our local number, so you could make an appointment beforehand and we'd be able to see you . . .'

As Ben wiped his eyes, Lucy remembered something else she'd been taught in training. In certain circumstances, volunteers could always signpost people to other organisations that might be able to help.

'Ben – why don't you go along to Centrepoint? There's a branch not far from here you can walk to. It's in Whitechapel. They run hostels for young people and often help them to find work. I'll scribble the directions for you now . . .'

'Oh, thanks, that *would* be great.' Ben sighed, gratefully sipping the cup of tea Lucy had made him.

After he left, Lucy felt a warm glow envelop her. She'd not only helped by just listening to what she'd been told but she'd also been able to suggest something practical too.

But there was more.

She felt she'd passed a personal test as well. In her heart of hearts, she'd wondered how she would fare actually facing someone in person. The phone, after all, acted as a kind of psychological barrier, protection even, against too much intimacy.

This last encounter though had boosted her confidence enormously.

Perhaps now was the time to challenge her mother further?

The next day, she was on duty again, doing her normal eight-to-ten-thirty shift.

Ambrose was her partner that day and wasn't engaged on a call himself when Alison rang . . .

ALISON

Maura would be wondering where I'd gone, so I sent her a text and told her I'd left the lounge to visit a chemist on the main concourse. 'Flu lingers' was the way I put it. It sounded a bit feeble, but as an excuse it would have to do.

After I'd left the cloakroom, I found a quiet corner in one of the main lounges and took out my phone again.

I couldn't get Lucy at first and began to worry – she might be on a long call and not be available, but eventually, after I'd tried several times, she answered. By now, I was breathless.

'I know I shouldn't be doing this, ringing you on duty, but I just *had* to. Something's just happened . . . I can't cope . . .'

'Alison . . .'

'*Please* let me talk! I'm having a panic attack! Can't cope . . . don't think I'm capable of catching the flight either.'

'Calm *down*, Alison. I understand but, look, someone . . . I'll call you from home later?'

The phone went dead.

I was stunned. Of course, I shouldn't have rung her when she was on duty but she was a friend – a special friend – and I needed her!

Feeling like a zombie, I walked back to the lounge. Maura and Trooper were laughing, leaning towards each other, sharing a joke. I hesitated. No way would I be joining them. I noticed that he now wore a pair of half-moon spectacles, emphasising his respectability.

So I texted Maura and told her simply that I was going home.

It was the end of the line really. I would never be able to go back to my job now. The wounds I'd hoped had long since healed lay raw and open once again.

I knew it wasn't rational, but I felt that Lucy had let me down. Duty or no duty, we should have talked. She'd rejected me!

I walked out of the airport and caught a cab home, just remembering to reclaim my luggage.

I sent Maura an email, saying I was resigning immediately. I explained that I'd been suffering from depression for some time and needed urgent medical attention.

I was trapped. My feelings of despair increased as the cab crawled its way back to central London in heavy traffic. What awaited me there, now that my life had collapsed?

Psychologically, the existence I'd attempted to create by reinventing myself had collapsed. Resignation swept over me. This was my fate and I had to be content that the good times had lasted as long as they had.

There was no future for me any more. I began to think of some means of escape. A plan was beginning to form in my mind . . .

LUCY

Ambrose sometimes listened to other volunteers on duty when he happened to be in the branch. As Director, he felt he should do this from time to time, just to ensure that the quality of the service was being maintained.

In any event, Lucy was new – still on probation, in fact – so listening in to her calls would be a perfectly natural thing to do. One morning, he picked up the spare headset attached to her phone.

Lucy sounded worried, shocked even, and, catching Ambrose's eye, looked furtive.

'Calm *down*, Alison. I understand but, look, someone . . . I'll call you from home later?'

She put her phone down suddenly.

Shaking his head, Ambrose disconnected it by taking it off its cradle.

'Lucy, did you know that person you'd just been speaking to?' he asked.

'Yes. She's a friend. I know she shouldn't have rung me here but –'

'No, she shouldn't! You also offered to ring her back when you got home as well. Has she ever been one of our callers?'

'No – well, yes, originally, but we're friends now . . .'

Ambrose was angry.

'Lucy, you know that's against all the rules. Personal involvement with any of our callers is absolutely forbidden. You were told that when you joined! Where are you going now?'

Lucy had risen from her chair, muttering, before rushing out of the room and into the corridor. Ambrose followed and found her fumbling with her mobile phone.

'Lucy, stop that!' he barked. 'You're about to ring that friend back, aren't you? I absolutely forbid it. It's a matter of principle!'

'Ambrose, she *needs* me,' Lucy cried. 'She's really upset!'

'That's as maybe!' he shouted. 'You're on duty *here,* remember? Now, calm down and come back into the duty suite. Other callers will be waiting.'

But as he stalked back, he began to have second thoughts. Whatever the rights and wrongs of the situation, he'd been much too harsh with Lucy, who was still relatively inexperienced. Was this how any Samaritan should behave? He of all people, as a director, should know better, he thought wryly, in failing to support a volunteer who had veered off the beaten track.

Intending to apologise, he was about to go out to find Lucy when the phone rang. Lucy's duty partner waved in his direction.

'Oh, Ambrose, I'm bursting for a pee. Could you possibly take that call for me?'

Ambrose nodded. 'Of course. Off you go. Let's hope Lucy will be back soon as well.'

It turned out to be a forty-five-minute call, during which, Ambrose noted, Lucy had failed to return.

After the shift ended, he checked to see whether she was still on the premises but there was no sign of her.

He sighed, making himself a coffee before going home and contemplating what action he should take. She might have been upset but she *had* abandoned her shift and her duty partner. At the very least, she could have come back and offered some explanation for her behaviour.

Perhaps it was appropriate to give her some space and wait to see what happened. In due course, she might very well contact him, but if not he'd give her a ring himself in the next few days.

Frantically, Lucy examined her phone for Alison's number, only to discover it wasn't there. Then she remembered: she'd left her phone at home the last day they'd met and Alison had scribbled it instead on a business card. The card wasn't in her purse but probably at home in another bag somewhere.

Now she had no alternative but to wait before trying Alison again when she got home. She'd made up her mind – she couldn't leave her friend in the lurch any longer. She'd have to face the consequences of quitting her duty.

Just as she was about to leave the premises, she ran into Gerald.

'Hi, Lucy, how are you?' Gerald's grin turned into a look of concern at Lucy's distressed face. 'You seem really upset. Can I help at all?'

Lucy pondered. To get home she'd have to either walk or wait for a bus.

'Oh, Gerald, I'm not sure . . . But . . . why are you here? You quit the course some time ago.'

A soon as she said it, it felt as if she was being nosy but Gerald didn't seem to mind.

'Oh, nothing important. The thing is, the first time I came here, I brought a book about counselling with me and left it behind somewhere on the premises. But that can wait. Tell me what's bugging you – only if you want to, of course.'

Lucy's eyes filled with tears. His kindness contrasted so markedly with Ambrose's uncompromising attitude.

'It's this friend of mine, Alison. She *was* a caller to begin with, it's true, but now much more than that! I need to get home and call her as quickly as possible.'

Breathlessly, she explained what had happened and her confrontation with Ambrose. Gerald shook his head in disbelief.

'Sounds to me as if Ambrose is too fixated on the rule book! You *must* try and help your friend now, in any way you can. How are you intending to get home?'

'Well, I'll walk or wait for a bus . . .'

'Nonsense! I'll take you there in my car. It's on a yellow line too, so there's no time to waste!'

Lucy was impressed by Gerald's gleaming black car – a Jaguar XL – smelling the rich aroma of the ivory-coloured leather as she settled in her seat. At any other time she would have relished this trip but her anxiety about Alison gnawed away at her all the way to the Barbican.

As they drove along, Gerald was asking Lucy how she'd found the training after he'd left.

'Oh, it was great until recently. I got through it all, and started taking calls on my own.'

'Well done!' Gerald said. 'You know, I really didn't want to drop out, but it was the best thing in the end. What I've decided to do is to take up counselling instead – do it professionally, I mean. Not quite yet. I still work part-time, and am very much involved in doing up my new house at the moment. It's not far from here, actually. But counselling is in the back of my mind constantly. That's why I came in to get that book I'd left behind.'

'Being a Sam is so different though,' Lucy said. 'We don't try and help people in that way. Quite rightly – we're not professionals. *We* listen – *they* offload – and, sometimes, that gives them the chance to heal *themselves* as it were . . . Oh, God, I'm sorry, that sounds so pompous!'

Gerald marvelled at the way Lucy had matured since he'd first met her.

'Not in the least, Lucy. And you're absolutely right but I want to do more – be a lot more pro-active, if you like. Ah, here's the main door into your flats.'

They were in the middle of the Barbican and the roar of London's traffic had receded as Lucy climbed out of the car.

Gerald suddenly had an idea.

'Listen, Lucy, why not log my number into your phone? You may not be able to get hold of your friend now or, even if you did, you might want to meet somewhere in due course – go round to her place later today even. Now, I'm not really busy at the moment and can always give you a lift. Did you say she lived somewhere in the Docklands? We all live more or less in the same area.'

Lucy did as Gerald suggested, and then hurried into the building.

'Thanks so much, Gerald – you've been such a help!'

ALISON

———

Suicide . . .

The real issue was: what was the best way to do it?

Pills were dangerous. I'd read somewhere that overdosing didn't actually mean a slow comfortable slide into oblivion. For instance, a large quantity of paracetamol, the most common pain-killer, led some time later to excruciating pain and caused damage to vital organs like the liver, often resulting in a lingering death.

Hanging was too barbaric to contemplate.

Nor did I want to do anything that might trau-matise other people. For that reason, throwing myself off a bridge in front of a train or onto a busy road would be impossible.

I knew I wouldn't waver once I'd made up my mind. I wasn't close to any of my relatives and no one would miss me now that my mother was dead.

I felt quite calm, more content, even feeling a kind of happiness. A great weight would be lifted if I did it – the burden of tackling the complexities and frustrations of life on a daily basis. An escape from the debilitating unhappiness that had been grinding me down since Trooper had re-entered my life.

But the question remained: how was I going to do it, and where?

Then I had an idea.

I knew just the place in the depths of Sussex with high, sheer cliffs, notorious for suicides.

Beachy Head.

A trip on the train, a taxi ride to the cliffs, then a leap – although I couldn't picture myself actually taking the plunge.

Into the unknown . . .

And afterwards . . .

What did death really mean to me?

There'd be no way back after that. So I had to be ready. Somehow it seemed wrong to act on an impulse. I needed a change of environment to help me find the courage to actually do the deed.

So I went online to look for a suitable hotel in the area where I could stay. Just somewhere to settle for a short period, to prepare . . .

There was an ideal place, within a couple of miles of the famous cliffs, run by a Frank Bedver and his wife Alice. Bedver's, once an ancient hostelry according to the blurb, was a small hotel near Eastbourne with twelve comfortable en-suite rooms.

Next to the details of the hotel were pictures of the cliffs, a visitor's centre and a map showing the distance to the coast was only three-quarters of a mile.

Another picture showed people dotted round a vast greensward spreading inland from the edge of the cliffs.

I rang to book, hoping I could have the spacious room at the back overlooking a lawn bordered by a bed filled with rose bushes.

Unfortunately, that room was already booked but there was one next door with a partial view of the garden, so I had to be content with that.

I left home and caught a train to Eastbourne and took a cab to the hotel. In order to allay any suspicion, I carried a backpack with a pair of walking boots attached to a strap, as well as a small case. If anyone were to ask, I was a keen walker anxious to explore the surrounding countryside by foot.

Frank Bedver was behind the desk when I arrived at the hotel. I booked in for a week. I would choose the actual day for the inevitable during that time. In the meantime, I would try to relax by exploring a part of the country I'd never visited before.

It might seem strange as I was about to die but I aimed to try for 'normal' as long as possible.

'Ah, good afternoon, Miss Hock.' The hotelier spoke with a soft Sussex burr.

'You're most welcome to our small establishment. Good news. Our best room, the one you wanted, has become available at short notice. I did send you a card but, knowing the post, you probably haven't received it. Just to remind you of our mealtimes: breakfast between eight and ten, bar lunches only between twelve and two and we start serving dinners at seven o'clock, with a good range of home-cooked meals. Menu's in your room upstairs. Nice view over the garden too. We hope you enjoy your stay with us.'

The room was indeed charming. Oak beams ran across the ceiling and maritime pictures adorned the wall. A little plaque indicated that a Captain Bedvent, a famous Eastbourne smuggler in the eighteenth century, had once lodged there for several weeks. I couldn't help smiling at the quaintness. Perhaps the Bedvers had put it up because of the similarity of their names. The novelty of my new surroundings kept me calm and distracted me from any darker thoughts.

After arriving, I contemplated going for a walk but, as it was a dull and misty day, I soon abandoned the idea. In fact, for the next few days, I stayed in my room or in the lounge downstairs, watching TV intermittently, listening to the radio, but mainly reading.

As a thirteen-year-old, I'd read almost the entire works of Agatha Christie and now, once again, immersed myself again in her nostalgic world of country-house charm tinged with malice.

Then one morning, Lucy rang . . .

LUCY

After Gerald dropped her off, Lucy searched for the business card but couldn't find it anywhere. She could only assume that she'd either dropped it in the street or thrown it away by accident.

Really worried now, she couldn't help thinking about Alison's last call and the desperate tone of her voice. How could she get in touch with her now? She didn't have an address.

Then she remembered a particular feature of the card. She'd glanced at it at the time, and vaguely recalled that the firm that employed Alison had a foreign-sounding name and started with a 'K' – Kapp, Kapper? – something like that. Apart from that, all she could remember was that the company was involved in cosmetics.

She duly entered 'cosmetic companies' into the search engine of her computer. A name might come up that would jog her memory.

Minutes later, she found what she was looking for. She was pretty sure that Alison's company was called '*Klephts* Kosmetics'. Now it was only a question of persuading them to divulge Alison's personal details, including her phone number.

That didn't prove easy at first. As she expected, the receptionist at the firm wouldn't give out the personal details of staff. Eventually, though, Lucy did persuade the woman to put her through to Alison's former boss, Maura.

After introducing herself, Lucy said, 'I know you wouldn't normally give out personal information, but I do believe it's more than justified here. Let me explain . . .'

Lucy bit her lip for a second, as the solemnity of the Samaritans' view on confidentiality gave her pause. How could she explain why she felt so anxious about Alison?

'I'm *really* worried about her, you see. I have reason to know that she's extraordinarily vulnerable at the moment. I'm sorry but you'll just have to trust me on this. At least, can you tell me: has she been into work at all?'

There was a slight pause before Maura replied.

'Well, no. Actually, she resigned immediately after deserting me at the airport. I haven't seen her since then.'

'The *airport* . . . ?'

'Sorry, I ought to explain. She was my PA and we were about to go to New York together on business. We were waiting for our flight, and she suddenly rushed off. It was odd really – just after I invited this doctor to come over and join us. The heart surgeon who saved that pop singer's life. I'd met him at a dinner previously and –'

'Was his name Trooper by any chance?'

'Yes – the one that's been in the news – bit of a celebrity now that he's written that book.'

'Oh God. She knew him! It will have brought everything back to her. Something terrible happened to her back then and he was involved. *Please* give me her number. I *must* speak to her urgently.'

After a second's hesitation Maura divulged the number. Lucy dialled it straight away.

ALISON

—

'Thank God you've answered, Alison. I've been so worried about you. How are you?'

I felt sullen resentment well up inside me.

'Why do you care? I really needed to talk when I rang that last time, thinking you were a friend but you cut me off!'

'I'm so sorry, Alison . . . but I *couldn't* . . . Ambrose was listening in at that exact moment. Don't forget I was on duty and –'

'Who's Ambrose?'

'The Director of my branch, the person in overall charge. As you know, it's against the rules to make friends with callers, and become emotionally involved with them.'

I thought for a moment. This was true, and I was certainly partially to blame for things changing between us, being so much older than Lucy.

'But we *did* become friends, didn't we, Lucy? I helped you face up to your sexuality. And you promised to ring me back later and didn't . . . not that it makes any difference now.'

'What are you saying, Alison?'

She might as well know.

'Quite simply, I've decided to end my life. Please don't try and talk me out of it. That's not the Samaritan way, is it? Remember those chats we had together about your rules!'

'Alison! *Please . . .*'

'"Self-determination", wasn't that the word you used? I can do what I want, after all. I feel my life's finished now. Please don't ring this number again. There won't be an answer.'

Cutting her off, I sighed and placed my mobile on a chest of drawers. Later, I would get rid of it somewhere. Then I crawled back into bed, pulling the covers up to my ears.

After almost a week, the clouds had gone, the sun was shining and I was ready. The very fact that it was so beautiful made it the obvious day to carry out my plan. The good weather was bound to bring people out in droves, and the sight of them enjoying themselves would only intensify my own misery.

I told the hotel I was going for a long walk, but would be back for dinner, determined not to give any hint of my true intentions.

I had to be prepared in case my courage failed me. So I had a thermos filled with the hotel's coffee, adding to the mix a generous proportion of vodka I'd bought with me.

I put in pills as well, a mixture of the Diazepam and a large amount of sleeping pills regularly prescribed for my mother at one time, but never used after she fell ill.

I placed the thermos and my backpack on the chest of drawers next to the mobile I'd forgotten about in the interim. Unthinkingly, I stuffed that, a bottle of water and some tissues into the backpack too.

When I reached the cliffs, the day was already growing warm. The grass looked freshly washed where the morning dew hadn't quite disappeared. Beyond the cliffs, the sea and horizon blended together in a haze of misty blue. Groups of visitors were strolling in the sunshine; some were beginning to sit on the grass, laying out picnics. I found a place to sit too, choosing a spot a reasonable distance away from anyone else.

I took long pulls from the flask until it was almost empty. Gradually, I began to feel intoxicated and tranquillised, and entered a druggy world of unreality . . .

After a while, exhilaration seeped over me. I was suddenly free of all concerns, the tight knot of tension in my stomach had gone. I breathed in deeply, savouring the freshness of the soft wind for the last time.

Standing up, I found myself staggering towards the cliffs, my body propelling itself forward automatically. Even before I reached the edge, I felt the emptiness reaching out to me . . .

LUCY

———

Lucy was devastated. She couldn't, just *couldn't*, abandon her friend. What she needed to do now was talk to her face to face.

Once again, Lucy rang Maura.

'I'm sorry to trouble you again, but I need more information. I did get through to Alison, but the situation is actually worse than I thought. This time, she sounded even more desperate than before. I need to go and see her. Can you give me her address?'

Maura sounded reluctant.

'Well, I'm not sure I should. It is confidential information, after all. I stretched a point giving you her phone number in the first place . . .'

'I know, but *please*, I *must* get hold of her!'

'She might have left home for all we know – could be anywhere really – but still, I *am* concerned about her welfare. She was such a good employee and up and left *so* unexpectedly. I'll go and fetch her address from our records. I'd come myself but we're very busy with a fashion shoot at present.'

'No, that's fine. I'll manage. Thanks so much for offering. I'll let you know when I find her.'

Lucy already knew what she was going to do. She'd ask Gerald to take her to the address.

Gerald and Lucy drove directly to Alison's address, a flat not far away, situated in Shoreditch.

The building was a former terrace house that had been converted into two flats with separate entrances, directly off the street. After trying the doorbell without success, they pondered what to do.

'She's gone away. I was warned,' Lucy said wearily.

Alison's letterbox was stuffed with circulars and flyers that hadn't been properly inserted, so Lucy extracted them, intending to push them back again. As she did so, a card fell to the ground, with a scrawled message on the back.

Picking it up, an address on it printed in bold black letters caught her attention.

BEDVER'S HOTEL, BEACHY HEAD

Lucy thought for a moment.

'So *that's* where she's gone!' she gasped, passing the card to Gerald.

'We need to find her, Lucy – if we can. Let's set off immediately!'

They drove down to Sussex and took the road to Eastbourne. It was still quite early in the morning so they hoped to arrive at Beachy Head by lunchtime.

During the journey, Lucy phoned the hotel and the proprietor, Frank Bedver, confirmed that Alison had been a guest there for a few days. She'd gone out only that morning for a long walk, but *who* were they, and *why* were they ringing?

'Oh, we're friends but very concerned about her. She's been going through a rough patch recently, and we're worried about what she might do. She's switched her mobile off too, you see. How has she seemed to you?'

Bedver took a moment before answering.

'Well, she's come across as a perfectly normal guest to us here. Quiet lady, stayed in her room most of the time while the weather's been bad. But today she set off with a thermos of coffee after a good breakfast, saying she's going to do some real walking. She looked fit and happy enough to me, I must say. The weather's improved, you see.'

'Did she say when she'll be back?'

'This evening. She'll be having her dinner here as usual. Do you want me to tell her you called?'

'No. We'll wait at your hotel until she gets back, except – Well, if you were to hear anything perhaps you'll ring us back on this number?'

'Will do, although I'm sure there's no reason to worry.'

ALISON

Whatever the paramedics had given me in the ambulance had knocked me out and now I was coming to in a hospital ward. A man in a white coat was standing over me. He was smiling as my eyes fluttered open.

'Ah, glad to have you back. Now, don't worry. I'm just checking you over: heartbeat, blood pressure, vital obs – that kind of thing. Just keep still.'

Groaning a little, I made to move my hand to my arm, which felt very sore. Gently, the doctor patted it away.

'Best not to touch that at the moment. It's broken but we'll soon be treating it and sorting out a cast for you.'

'Where am I?'

'A&E, Eastbourne General Hospital. I'm the duty doctor here. Your arm isn't badly fractured fortunately. You were very lucky in *where* you happened to fall, you know, and that your injuries weren't more serious.'

I was only half listening, my mind still in a fug of shock, although gradually things were coming back to me.

Intoxicated, I'd closed my eyes as I prepared to jump, savouring the whoosh of air that washed over me on the edge of the cliff.

Opening them, I saw the red-and-white-striped lighthouse below me, swaying, wobbling and trembling in front of my eyes, and then dipping alarmingly as I teetered on the brink. It was such a long way down, and visceral fear suddenly gripped me; fear of my body being smashed against the rocks and a deeper fear that what I intended to do was wrong, so very wrong.

Events flashed through my mind that I hadn't thought about for years. Sunday School lessons I'd gone to as a child; Religious Education classes, part of the syllabus in the 1960s, which I'd been forced to attend reluctantly, as a teenager.

It was always wrong to end your life by your own hand. It was a sin, as life was given to you by God.

These thoughts must have buried themselves deep into my unconscious when I'd originally asked Samaritans for help and received it so generously and without hesitation.

That help would have continued had I not taken advantage of Lucy and tried to keep her to myself – landing *her* in all sorts of trouble.

This was unforgivable. She was so much younger than me, a woman in late middle age, while she was essentially still a girl and susceptible to influence.

I'd make it up to her somehow. We could remain a part of each other's lives if she could accept our being friends. But she could no longer act as a Samaritan for me.

But there were always other people available to talk to twenty-four hours a day – just for times like this when my feelings were threatening to overwhelm me.

Life beckoned me once more. I took a step backwards.

At that moment, the chalky ground beneath my feet began to crumble. I flung my arms out in desperation, but it was too late. I was going to be smashed on the rocks below! Then I landed on a ledge a few feet down. The crunch and thump of my body hitting solid ground stunned me for a moment before the intense pain in my arm started. Fortunately, it had taken the brunt of the fall. I could still just see the lighthouse, which was partially hidden by the ledge that had saved my life.

I was still wearing the backpack. Scrabbling inside it, I managed to locate my mobile phone and dial 999.

After the nurses had put the cast on my lower arm and I'd been issued with a sling, all I wanted was to be discharged and go back home.

But first, I ordered a taxi to take me back to the hotel in order to settle their bill and pick up my things.

Just as I was struggling into my scuffed and dirty clothes, the doctor visited me once more. I noticed now the lines of strain etched on his face and how exhausted he looked, yet he was still able to talk to me gently and calmly.

'Miss Hock, you're free to leave at any time, of course, but I would suggest that you speak to our hospital social worker, Verity, first. After all, you were attempting to take your life by jumping off that cliff and –'

'No! Sorry, that's not what really happened. I mean I was thinking along those lines but –'

Should I tell him the real truth? Would he even believe me if I did?

Sensing my hesitation, he patted my hand.

'Don't upset yourself, Miss Hock, by discussing it with me. Instead have a word with Verity before you go. She *is* a trained counsellor.'

As he awaited my reply, a nurse approached and spoke to him. Turning back to me, he said, 'Miss Hock, it appears you have visitors – a Miss Vanser and Mr Redland. Would you like to see them now?'

For the very first time since the accident, emotion overcame me.

Lucy was here!

'Yes. Oh, yes,' I sobbed.

Lucy and Gerald

When they reached the main road to Eastbourne, the cars in front of them ground to a standstill. A radio report told them that the road ahead was blocked due to a serious traffic accident and they would have to take alternative routes.

As they crawled at a snail's pace along side roads, they both began to feel increasingly tense.

'At this rate, we won't get to Beachy Head until well into the afternoon,' Lucy said plaintively, 'by which time she might actually have *jumped*. Oh, Gerald, what *can* we do?'

Gerald gritted his teeth, as the cars in front of him stopped moving for several minutes.

'Nothing. We'll just have to be patient, that's all.'

The traffic had eased slightly when Lucy's mobile buzzed. She snatched it from her lap.

'Yes. Mr Bedver. Oh God! You mean she's actually done it!'

Gerald swiftly indicated left into a small layby, causing the car behind to hoot furiously, before he brought his own vehicle to a shuddering halt.

'Sorry?' Lucy said breathlessly. 'I couldn't quite hear you, the reception's bad. Could you repeat that? She *attempted* – so they've found her! She's still alive then. But how badly injured?'

Gerald switched off the ignition.

'I understand. All you know at present is that she's been taken to Eastbourne General Hospital . . .'

Gerald tapped the information into his satnav, before starting the engine.

'We'll go straight there, Lucy.'

REDRESS

Somehow during the book signing he'd held it together.

In fact, the event had gone on longer than anticipated because of the long queues stretching right out into the street and, at least, it meant that the fear had been pushed out of his mind for a time.

But now the dread returned with a vengeance.

Somebody, somewhere out there, had that laptop. It would probably be sold on quickly but it could only be a matter of time before the files were discovered and examined. The stuff hadn't even been protected with a password.

He'd kept that computer locked in a cupboard, but the thief or thieves had been expert and ransacked his flat efficiently and thoroughly.

What they found in there would ruin him forever. The pictures of young girls, semi-clothed or naked, the lewd posturing of their abusers . . .

His sordid, secret passion revealed to the world.

Now, he stopped off at a pub just off Leicester Square and downed a whisky. Then several more.

Feeling woozy, he made his way to Piccadilly station. The rush hour was still at its height. The concourse at the bottom of the escalators was packed with people pressing through the access tunnels to the platforms.

He stood for a moment wondering. Today, he was famous, respected and revered – with a knighthood into the bargain. A letter from the Cabinet Office had confirmed it only this morning.

But tomorrow . . .

Blackmail was a real possibility. Exposure . . . shame . . . maybe even prison.

Some of the images he'd viewed and stored over the years were the most explicit of their kind. It had all begun with curiosity but he'd soon become addicted, and then there'd been no way back.

He pushed through the crowd and jostled his way to the edge of the platform . . .

ALISON

I woke up, still feeling groggy from the pills I'd taken the day before, on top of the painkillers the hospital had given me, but realised eventually that I was in a hotel bedroom.

My arm in its cast still throbbed slightly but I'd grown used to it by now, and generally felt a whole lot better after a good night's sleep.

As I rather clumsily made myself a coffee, memories of the previous day started coming back to me in glimpses . . .

Lucy arriving at the hospital, accompanied by a man she introduced as Gerald, a former trainee at her branch; my state of emotional collapse on seeing her, illustrated by the fact that I couldn't stop crying; apologies on my part for what I appeared to have done – or not done – eventually explaining what really happened and how, in the end, it really had been an accident . . .

Neither of them interrupted as I recounted my tale.

Having got it off my chest, which brought great relief, I was determined to stick to my original plan and go home as soon as I could. As I started to struggle into my clothes with the help of the nurses, I saw that Lucy and Gerald had gone into a huddle.

They'd come up with a plan and were determined to take me back to London, but not until the next day, due to my condition. Gerald spelled out the details.

First, having cancelled the taxi, we were going back to Bedver's to pick up my things, before driving into Eastbourne, where we would stay the night in a luxury hotel called the Salisbury situated on the seafront.

'But you don't have any night things!' I protested when Gerald told me.

'We've already discussed that and our plans for the night. I've already booked three rooms – which I will pay for by the way. No arguments – it will be my treat to you both. You need a bit of molly-coddling after your experience, and Lucy is exhausted – so am I for that matter!'

He smiled, which might have softened the air of authority that emanated from him but there was no doubt that he was used to having his decisions accepted without question.

I began to cry again.

'It's the best thing, Alison. You look all in, which isn't surprising when you think of what you've been through.' Gerald spoke more gently this time. 'So we'll take you to the hotel after popping in at Bedver's to get your stuff. It will be quite late by then, so why not just go to bed? Room service can always provide you with something to eat if you get peckish. In the meantime, we'll go off to some shops somewhere to purchase whatever we need to stay the night.'

The rest of the evening had gone according to plan, although it seemed like a blur now. The reality was, though, that I'd spend the night in a comfortable hotel and might as well make the most of it.

The Salisbury was very well appointed, with magnificent bathrooms, separate showers and all the little luxuries provided by a good hotel: bars of scented soap, and little bottles containing shampoo and bath foam. A fluffy robe with matching slippers had also been laid out next to the bed.

As I padded about the room, I found a note, written on the hotel's crested notepaper, pushed under the door. It was from Lucy.

Hi Alison,
There's no rush in the morning – if you want breakfast why not order it from room service?

– unless you decide to come down and join us instead. Otherwise, why not relax in your room and contact us when you're ready? We're in Rooms 104 and 105 on the same floor, so near you in 109. We could join you for a coffee and a chat if you'd like that.

Hope you had a good night's rest –

Lucy

After using the bathroom, I checked the time by glancing at the clock radio next to the bed. It was still quite early and although Gerald and Lucy might not have gone down to breakfast as yet, I decided not to join them.

All I wanted to eat was some of the fruit provided by the hotel attractively displayed in a cut-glass bowl.

After sampling a couple of peaches, some grapes and a tangerine, I made another cup of coffee and settled back in bed.

I needed time to myself to think before seeing anyone at all that day.

For a few moments, a deep sense of shame engulfed me – *why* had my self-esteem plummeted to these depths?

But further self-analysis or, for that matter, psychoanalysis undertaken by a professional wasn't the answer either. The real problem was that I'd suppressed my feelings of resentment, firstly about my father and most significantly about the rape itself, including the trial, and had never come to terms with these experiences at all.

That had led to my ultimate breakdown.

How I shaped my life from now on was the most important thing.

Sighing, I sat up in the bed. I could feel anxiety building up inside me once again and I knew it would be a mistake to rush into making any decisions too soon.

To distract myself, using the remote control, I switched on the flat-screen TV opposite the bed.

The main news on the BBC was all about the war in Syria and a recent bombing of a hospital in a rebel-held part of a large city. The terrible tragedy of that conflict distracted me so that I almost missed an item that appeared in the moving strapline at the bottom of the screen.

CELEBRITY DOCTOR EDWARD TROOPER'S TRAGIC DEATH YESTERDAY AT PICCADILLY CIRCUS UNDERGROUND STATION. POLICE ARE NOT EXCLUDING SUICIDE BUT SAY AN INQUEST WILL HAVE TO BE HELD TO DETERMINE HOW HE CAME TO FALL UNDER THE WHEELS OF AN INCOMING TRAIN.

I shot out of bed.

What did this mean? Did he fall under this train by accident or did he jump?

I could hardly wait for a fuller report to appear and later, in a bulletin, it did.

Trooper was seen by several passengers at the station pushing his way onto a crowded platform during the rush hour. Some witnesses, smelling alcohol, thought he might be drunk as he forced his way right to the front and stood just in front of the yellow safety line. Moments later, he was seen to fall beneath the wheels of an incoming train.

I switched off the TV and got out of bed in a daze, not quite taking it all in at first. Then euphoria swept over me . . .

Revenge! Justice *at last* for what he'd done to me all those years ago!

But then a profound sense of shame hit me. Looking for justice had never meant that I actually *wanted him to die* – particularly in such a horrible way.

My body began to shake uncontrollably as memories of the trial and all that had happened since swirled foggily in my mind. I had to sit down in an armchair, clawing at its arm with my free hand until my body finally began to relax.

Then the house phone on the table next to me rang. It was Lucy.

'Alison! Hope we're not ringing too early but . . . well, we were worried. You may not have heard the news today. It's about Trooper. He's been killed!'

Her actually saying it suddenly made me feel much better.

'Yes, I saw it. Thank you for warning me anyway, Lucy.'

'We've already had breakfast. Would you like us to come and see you?'

'Please, as soon as you're ready.'

Gently, I replaced the phone on its cradle and sighed.

Suddenly, so much of what had happened was beginning to lose its intensity. Trooper was dead and all I felt now was relief. But it did mean one thing for sure.

Closure.

GERALD AND LUCY

After talking things through in Alison's room over a coffee, the three of them decided not to linger in the Eastbourne area any longer. There was always a chance that the press might track Alison to get a story about her fall, and Lucy, in particular, was anxious to see her mother as soon as she could.

'She did try to ring me last night when she got home from work,' she informed the others. 'But I just texted her back to say I was staying the night with a friend. I just couldn't face talking to her then. But now I do need to get back home and try and make up. I *hate* rowing with my mum.'

Lucy had finally made up her mind that she wasn't resuming the Business Management course. Instead, without telling her mother, she'd already applied to study History instead at the University of Greenwich, just across the river.

Predictably, her mother was very upset.

'Oh, Lucy, I was really depending on you following me into the business and I thought – well, when you told me that you liked girls and I didn't make a fuss – that you'd do it for *me*, and to keep the firm going in your father's memory.'

Lucy suddenly remembered Alison's advice, that she needed to stand up to her mother more.

'Oh, for God's sake, Mum, it's got *nothing* to do with Dad's memory. He died years ago! It's really because of you wanting to run my life. That's got to change!'

Her mother rounded on her.

'If that's how you really feel, perhaps then it's time you moved out. You've grown up now, so find your own place to live!'

Lucy hadn't anticipated her mother taking such a hard line. Although she reckoned on being able to raise a loan to cover her tuition fees, she couldn't afford the cost of independent accommodation in London.

'Oh, Mum, you know how difficult it will be for me to do that! Can't you ever see things from my point of view?'

'Well, you'll have to decide: stick with me and the firm or go your own way!'

After this exchange, her mother flounced off to work, leaving Lucy feeling utterly bereft.

'Have you tried ringing her this morning, Lucy?' Alison now asked.

'I did try but she'd left home early, as she often does, and I don't want to disturb her at work.'

Gerald finished his coffee and rose to his feet.

'Well, let's all pack up then and get under way as soon as we can. I've already settled the bill downstairs.'

'Oh, Gerald, I really do feel I should contribute,' Alison protested. 'After all, I *am* responsible for dragging you both down here.'

Gerald waved his finger at her in mock disapproval. 'Now, Alison, remember what I said yesterday. It's my treat!'

During the journey, Alison suddenly felt hungry for the first time in hours. She hadn't ordered anything from room service the previous night either, and had eaten only fruit that morning.

But she was reluctant to ask Gerald to stop the car, feeling she'd caused enough inconvenience already and didn't want to cause any further delay. Besides, Lucy had grown quiet and wasn't very sociable, no doubt brooding over the row she'd had with her mother.

Twenty minutes later, Lucy's phone rang.

'Mum? Oh, Mum, I hadn't expected to hear from you until later. I've lots to tell you and – What?

You're sorry! *Oh*, Mum, so am *I*! Where am I? Actually in a car heading back to London. It's a long story but you did get my text? Oh, *good*. I'd love that. See you when you get home tonight. Bye.'

She returned the phone to her bag and let out a sigh of relief.

'Sorry about that. I didn't think I'd hear from her until much later in the day. She'd like us to go out for a meal to talk things over.'

'It's good that she rang,' Gerald said. 'Sounds like better news all round.'

'It *is*. All this time I've been worrying about Mum throwing me out any minute. I never expected her to come round to my way of thinking.'

With tears in her eyes, Lucy turned to Alison, who was sitting on the back seat.

'I have *you* to thank for that, Alison. You were *so* right when you told me that I had to make a stand!'

Before Alison could reply, Lucy began to wriggle in her seat. 'Oh, God. The excitement's really got to me. Gerald, do you think we can stop off somewhere? I've got to go to the loo!'

It was Alison's opportunity to make a suggestion of her own.

'I'll join you, Lucy. And, as we're stopping, Gerald, could we have something to eat as well? I'm absolutely starving!'

Gerald chuckled.

'I know *just* the place where the food's first class and we can break our journey at leisure.'

Alison didn't want to be a nuisance.

'Anywhere will do, Gerald – roadside café, snack bar somewhere – just to have a sandwich or something.'

'Nonsense, Alison. You need a good meal after your ordeal. That bit of fruit you had this morning wasn't nearly enough. Besides, I fancy having some fish – a speciality of the place where we're going. What about you, Lucy – are you hungry?'

Lucy patted her stomach. 'I ate a huge hotel breakfast, but there's always room for something more.'

'Good, that's settled then. We're on our way.'

The Felician Hotel and Restaurant was housed in a creeper-clad former manor house that nestled gently in a valley in the depths of Sussex. Its reputation for gracious country living depended more on word of mouth than overt advertising, and Gerald had often entertained clients there in the past.

ALISON

Strange as it might seem, real nourishment was just what I needed at that point and a rare fillet steak grilled to perfection and garnished with wild mushrooms and home-grown tomatoes, followed by chocolate profiteroles and cream, filled that need perfectly. Perhaps the trauma I'd suffered induced an atavistic craving for food now that the danger had gone.

Subsequently, while sipping a coffee in the hotel's luxuriously appointed lounge, feeling relaxed and content, a wave of affection for my two companions came over me, followed by a concern for Lucy's welfare. By this time, I'd had the chance to put my thoughts into some sort of order too.

Thanking Gerald, a complete stranger, after all, would be my first priority.

Then I had to do something for Lucy, who'd not only made such an effort to rescue me, but served her charity so well until I'd actually encouraged her to break the rules.

Alison

I had to try and put things right for her some-how before turning to my own needs . . .

GERALD

Gerald threw his keys down on the hall table.

His new house looked pristine now that the renovations both inside and outside were virtually complete and all the modern devices for daily living had been installed.

Yet none of that lifted his mood as he strode into his kitchen to make himself a cup of coffee. Instead, the pain of his loss gouged his heart more acutely than ever, despite there being nothing on the premises to remind him of Mel and Scarlett.

He knew this was bound to happen from time to time and was able to cope with it, but the events of the morning – how busy he'd been helping Lucy and Alison – emphasised his need to fill the void in his life with something positive as quickly as he could.

As he cut himself a large wedge of the whole Stilton he'd bought from a local delicatessen the day before, and put it on a plate with some fresh French bread, he reflected on the Samaritan training, and why, in the end, becoming a volunteer for that organisation hadn't been for him. He needed to be more involved, help people in a practical sense, using his managerial skills in a positive capacity. Just *listening* wasn't enough for him.

Pushing his plate aside, he realised what was really in his mind. He needed to find a different kind of career, a new profession altogether into which he could pour his energies. Simply making money no longer attracted him. His experience of the Samaritans, both as a client and a volunteer, had convinced him this time that he wanted to do something proactive to help people feel in control of their own lives.

All this must have been fermenting in the back of his mind when he'd returned to the centre to pick up his counselling book the very morning he'd run into Lucy.

He turned on his computer and searched for counselling and psychology courses.

LUCY

—•—

A few days later, Lucy and her mother, Sue, chose a quiet Italian restaurant within walking distance of their flat to eat and both agreed not to refer to their dispute until after the meal.

Afterwards, Sue spoke first.

'Something you said the other day struck home, Lucy. As you know, I've been working my socks off to keep Vanser Hotels going all these years, thinking that you'd want to follow me into the business and perhaps take it over even, in due course –'

'Mum, you never actually *asked* me if that's what I really wanted, did you?'

Sue raised her hand.

'Hear me out, Lucy. I've been thinking about that, believe you me, and I've come to the conclusion I was just deluding myself. You see, as you never *actually* said you *didn't* want to join the business, I just assumed you did. Then, the other day, you stood up to me for the first time ever and it brought me down to earth. I realised it was just being plain selfish, because that's what *I* wanted . . .

'So I've made some decisions. Firstly, you *must* be allowed to choose your own career and I shan't try to hinder you any longer. Secondly, I'm changing direction too. Vanser's has become very profitable and I'm intending to sell up. Recently, I've had several lucrative offers from large hotel chains to purchase the company and I'm going for it. The sale will make us, as a family, very well off, which means I'll finance you all the way in whatever you want to do. Indeed, I intend to do something different myself. As you know, I rarely watch any TV but, when I do, I love those animal programmes presented by David Attenborough. Well, I've decided to apply to the Open University to study zoology.'

Lucy felt a wave of affection come over her.

'Oh, Mum, that's great news! But going back to our row, now perhaps you understand why I *had* to have it out with you. It could be because I've learned a lot about myself since I joined Samaritans . . .'

She hesitated. It was on the tip of her tongue to tell her mother that she wasn't doing any duties at present and what had happened over Alison but thought better of it. It could wait for another day.

Her mother hadn't finished either.

'There *is* one other thing. I believe we both could do with a holiday, just the two of us. I'm sure the sandwich bar can spare you for a couple of days, so I've come up with an idea. Do you remember seeing that programme about Longleat, the stately home? Why don't we go down there and spend a couple of nights in a hotel nearby and go round the safari park to see the animals?'

'Perfect, Mum. Let's go as soon as possible!'

Her mother smiled. 'I think we'll have to wait until the sale of the business is finalised.'

A few days later, Ambrose rang and suggested they have a chat in the centre. Lucy wondered whether the purpose of this was really to let her go, so she decided to speak up first as soon as she arrived.

'I think I should resign, Ambrose. I broke the rules, I know, and as I'm about to go back to college, I may not have the time to continue anyway.'

There was a pause.

'That would be great pity, Lucy,' Ambrose said gently, 'because there have been some developments since I last saw you. First, I received a letter from your caller, Alison, explaining what really happened between the two of you. She made it clear that she felt she'd really inveigled you into becoming her friend, even though she knew it went against the way we do things here.'

Lucy shook her head vigorously. 'I . . . I knew what I was doing, and that it was wrong too!'

'True enough, but Alison feels she'd put you in an impossible situation, and for that she takes full responsibility.'

Lucy felt a wave of gratitude come over her. She'd been given no hint that Alison would choose to do anything like this nor had she spoken to her after they'd all returned to London. Alison had said she was looking forward to a short cruise but would be in touch after she'd returned.

'The second thing', Ambrose continued, 'was that Alison thanked us generally – the Sams as a whole, I mean – for our support but for yours in particular, Lucy. It was how *you* helped her from the *outset* that really changed her mind about jumping off that cliff at the last minute. You see, she told me everything in the end.'

Lucy began to detect a sense of well-being again.

Perhaps, she'd proved herself to be a worthy Samaritan after all.

Noticing that she'd begun to cheer up, Ambrose warned her, 'Don't allow yourself to become too confident, Lucy. You did break the rules and must promise never to do that again.'

Lucy nodded. 'I've learned my lesson, Ambrose.'

She was on the verge of tears.

'Oh God. How lucky Alison was. If she hadn't tumbled onto that ledge, it would have been too late!'

'Well, it wasn't. And there's another thing. Do you remember a girl called Willow, the one with the abusive father you were really worried about? You thought she might be actively suicidal but in fact she drew back from the brink and became a regular caller after she talked to you. She did get her life in some sort of order apparently.'

'Now, the dates don't matter, but she always remembers getting through to you initially, although as it turned out she doesn't actually think she spoke to you again. The fact is, though, that you started the process and she's written a note of thanks to you personally. She went to some trouble to deliver it to the centre, so must have got hold of our address somehow.'

He handed her a scrap of paper. As Lucy read it, her eyes filled with tears.

To the Samaritans, Wapping branch

I was really losing it the first time I rang. Almost took all the pills in front of me, but I didn't because talking to Lucy really helped. After I began to ring regular like and one of you was always there every time I picked up the phone, though I never got Lucy again. But she was the first and I'll always remember her lovely kind voice which got me talking. I had this problem with me dad, see. I told him it had to stop. Then it did, and he told the Social too, but went inside all the same. I dunno if I want to see him ever again but I got me life back with the help of Samaritans.

Best of wishes,
Willow

Ambrose leaned forward and pressed Lucy's arm. Then he smiled and said, 'Speaks for itself. What a good job you did. You know, you're more than welcome to come back to the branch as a volunteer. The truth is: you've been sorely missed. We can adjust your shifts to fit in with college.'

'Oh, thanks, Ambrose. That would be great!'

'There's still one last surprise to come, Lucy. In that letter I mentioned from Alison, she expressed a wish to become a Samaritan herself . . .'

EPILOGUE

The only sound in the room was the quiet steady hum of the computer accompanied by the flickering of the router, its popping dots dancing before her eyes.

London had been a ghost town when she'd left home in the early hours, the only inhabitants in the streets being cats and the rough sleepers, wrapped up and blanketed against their harsh tarmac world.

Alison glanced at the clock on the wall. Half-past three and still several hours of the night shift to go. A long-drawn-out haul during which the body was at its lowest ebb.

Until now, the callers had varied from people who were lonely and depressed to those clearly suffering from mental health problems, but there had been no suicidal calls as such.

A sweep of light from a passing car peeped through the closed curtain by the window on her right. She blinked and, just at that moment, the phone jangled.

She picked it up, her hand shaking slightly. It was, after all, her first night duty at the centre.

'Samaritans – can I help you?'

There was a long pause.

Then the sobbing . . .

She leaned back in her chair and took a deep breath. It was important to stay relaxed, to induce calm in the caller.

'I'm going to do it, cut my throat. The knife's in my hand.' A woman's voice.

Alison spoke slowly.

'I'm so glad that you decided to ring us. We are here to listen. You're through to the right place. Would you like to tell me what's been happening in your life to bring you to this?'

There was a sigh. Another long pause but she waited as all Samaritans are trained to do.

And then the caller began to talk . . .